THE GREAT PET ESCAPE

Victoria Jamieson

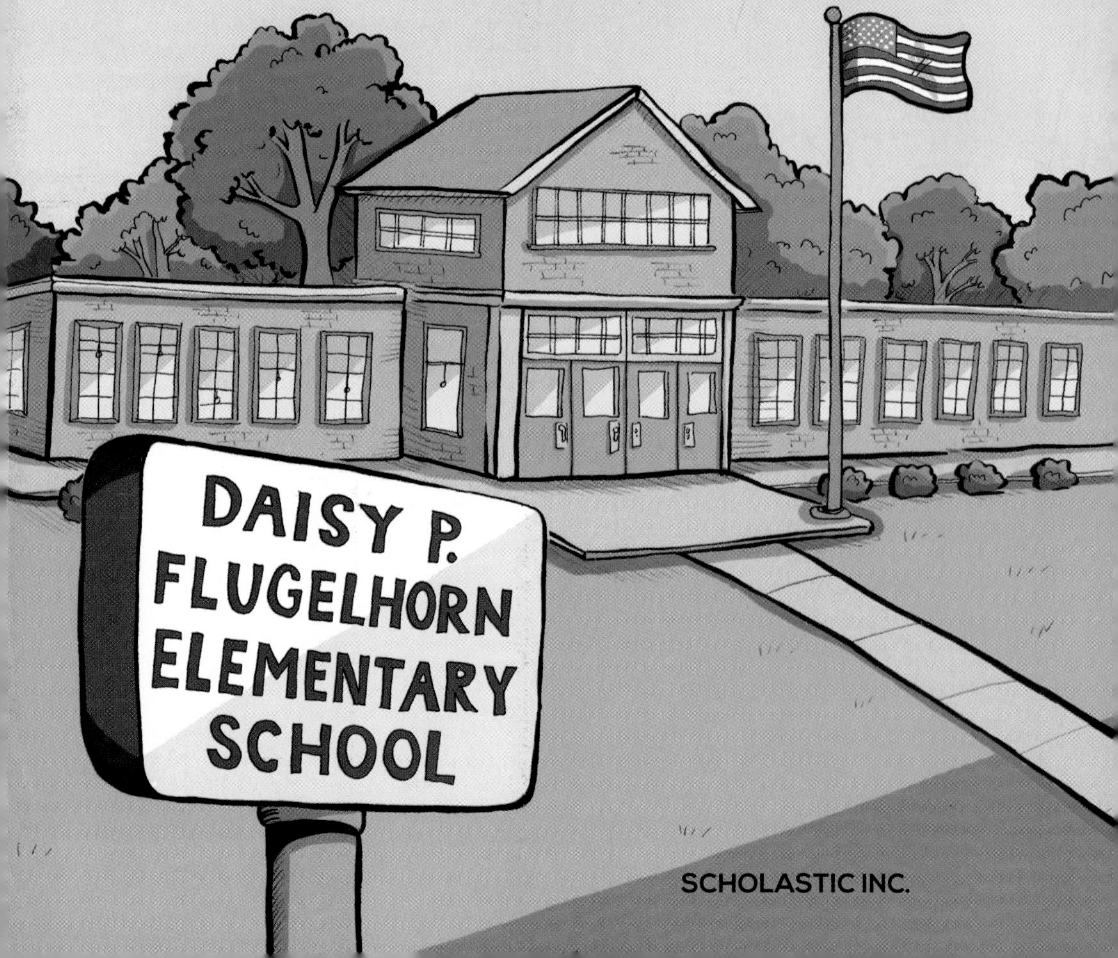
DAISY P.
FLUGELHORN
ELEMENTARY
SCHOOL

SCHOLASTIC INC.

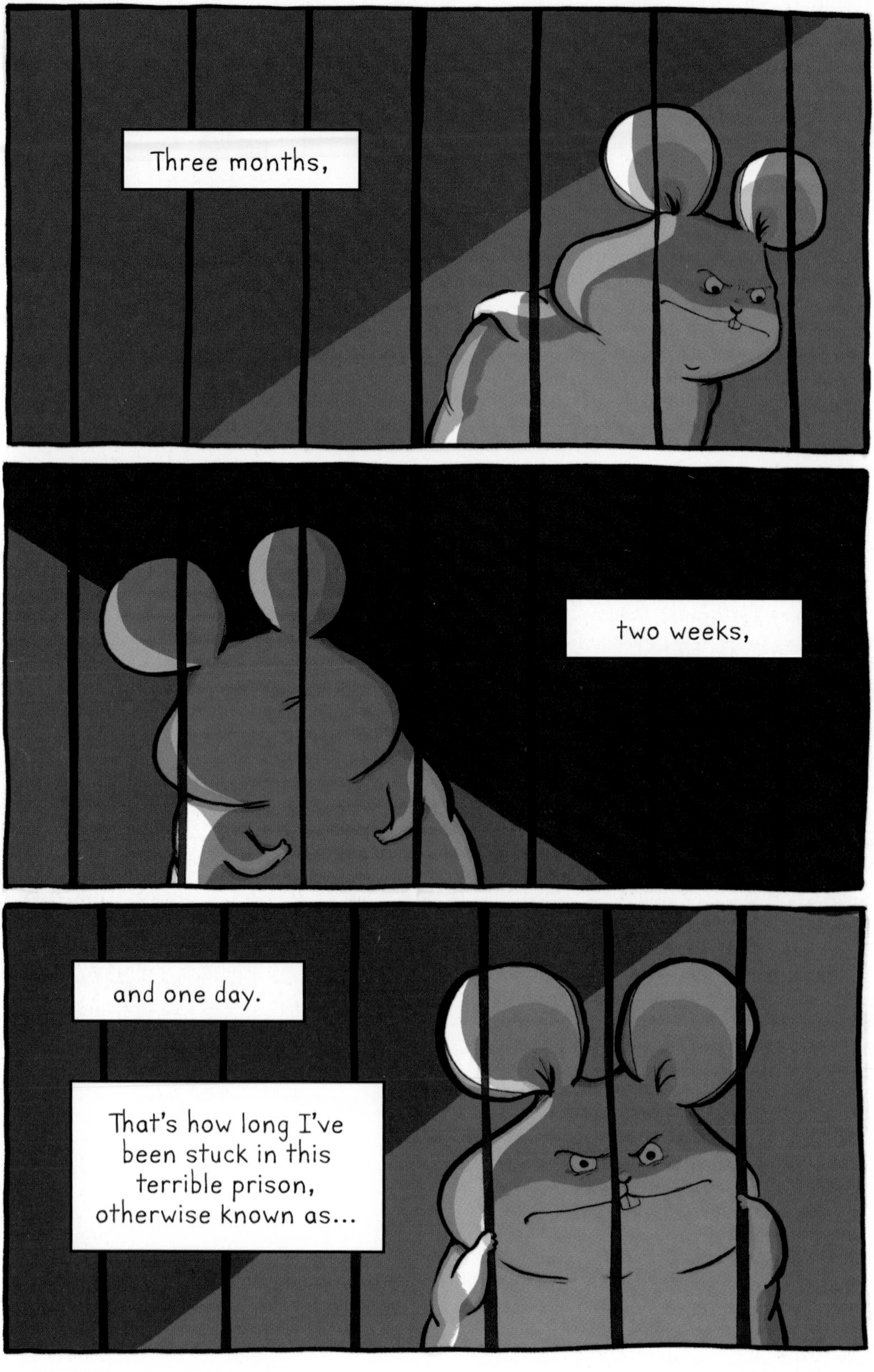
Three months,
two weeks,
and one day.
That's how long I've been stuck in this terrible prison, otherwise known as...

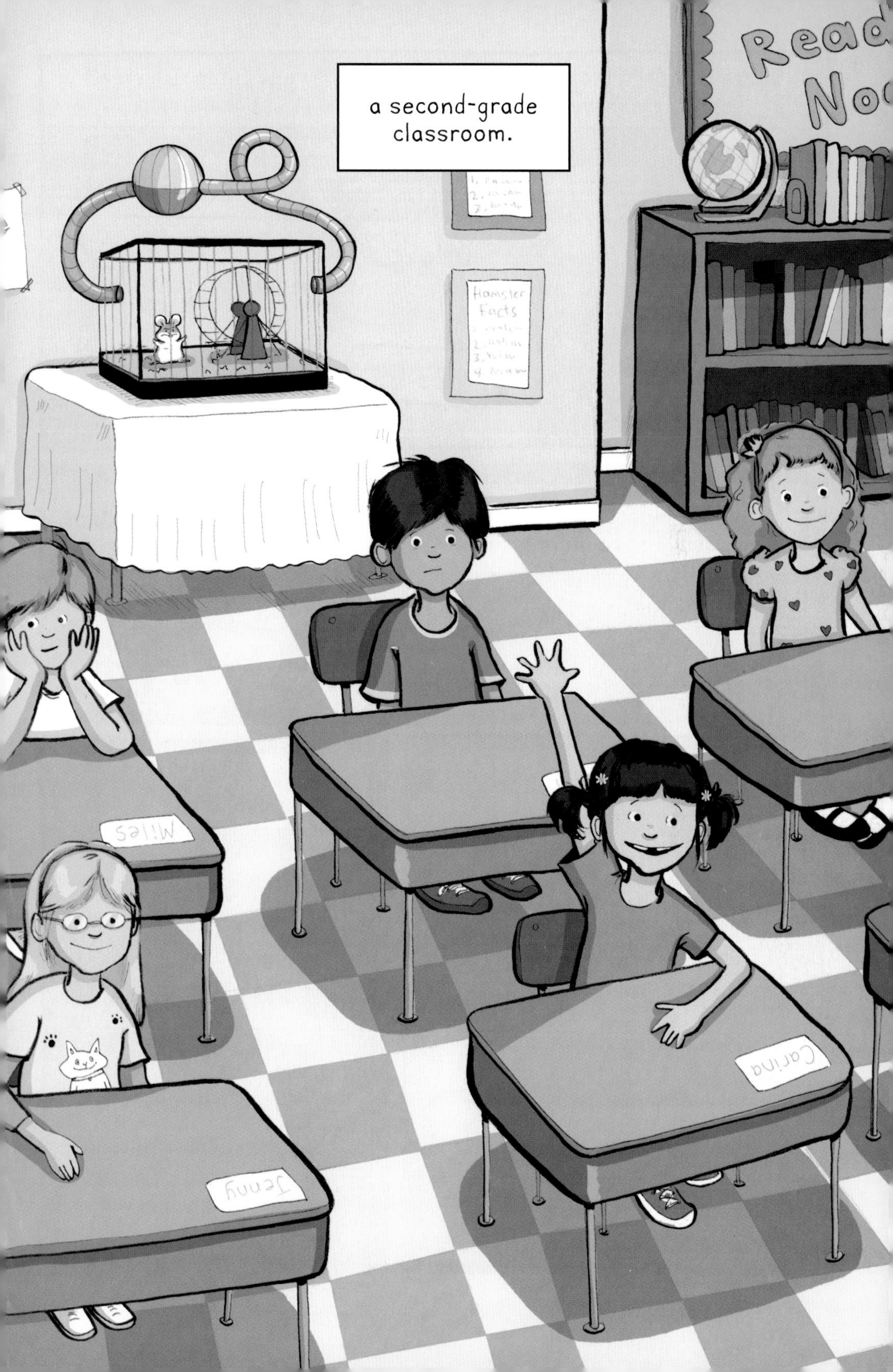
a second-grade classroom.
Hamster Facts
Miles
Carina
Jenny

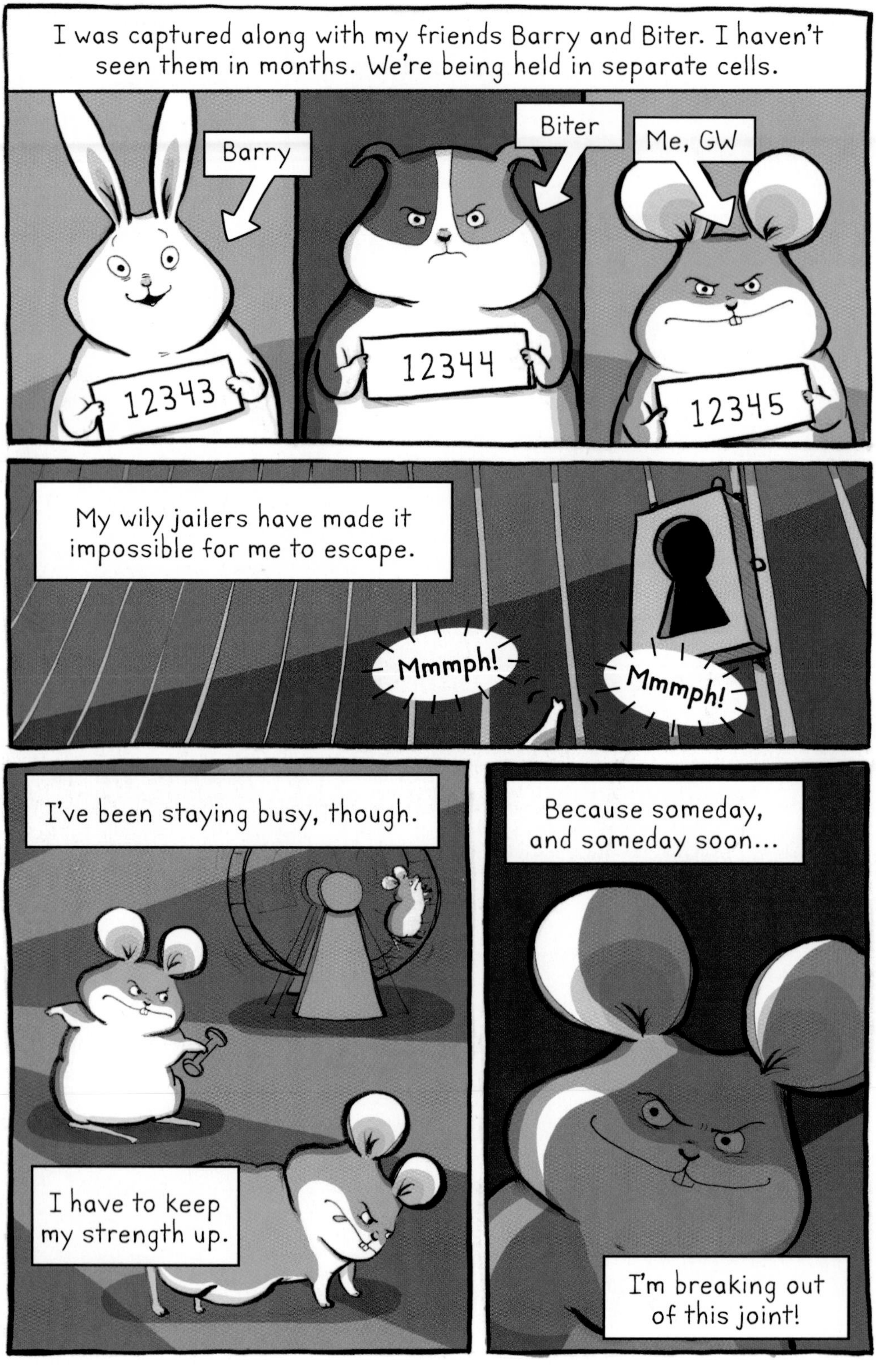
I was captured along with my friends Barry and Biter. I haven't seen them in months. We're being held in separate cells.
Barry
Biter
Me, GW
12343
12344
12345
My wily jailers have made it impossible for me to escape.
Mmmph!
Mmmph!
I've been staying busy, though.
I have to keep my strength up.
Because someday, and someday soon...
I'm breaking out of this joint!

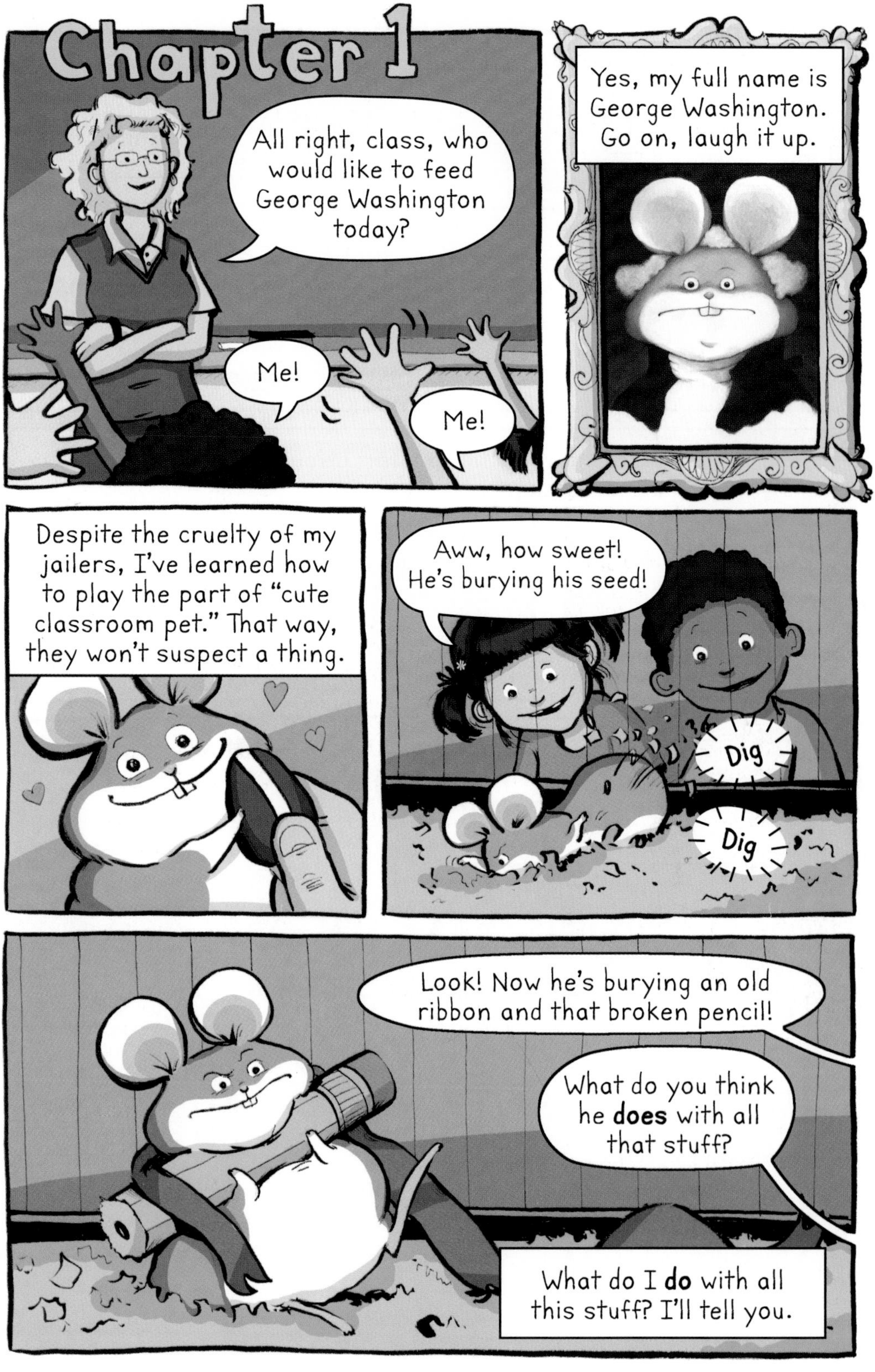
Chapter 1
All right, class, who would like to feed George Washington today?
Me!
Me!
Yes, my full name is George Washington. Go on, laugh it up.
Despite the cruelty of my jailers, I've learned how to play the part of "cute classroom pet." That way, they won't suspect a thing.
Aww, how sweet! He's burying his seed!
Dig
Dig
Look! Now he's burying an old ribbon and that broken pencil!
What do you think he **does** with all that stuff?
What do I **do** with all this stuff? I'll tell you.

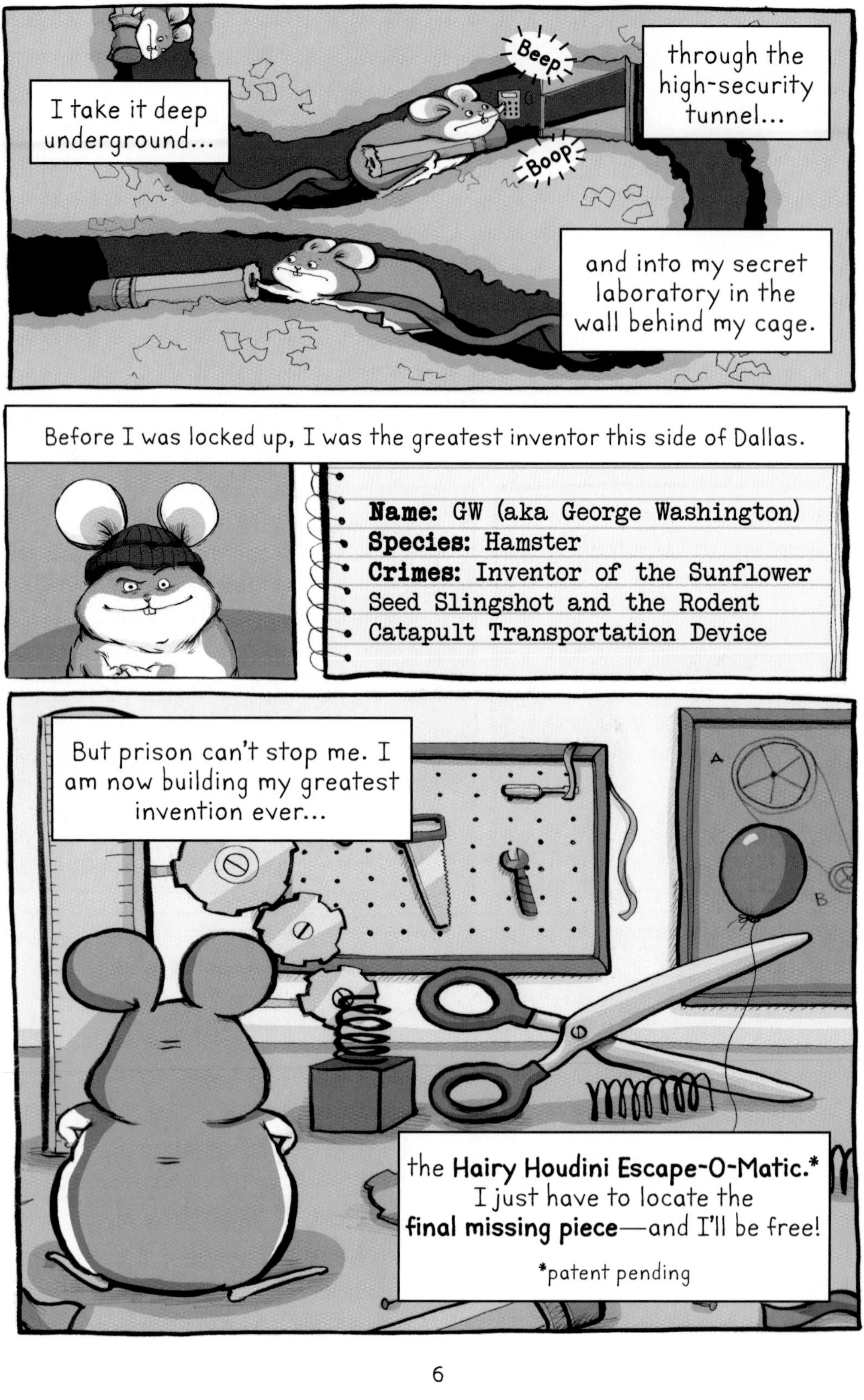
I take it deep underground...
Beep
Boop
through the high-security tunnel...
and into my secret laboratory in the wall behind my cage.
Before I was locked up, I was the greatest inventor this side of Dallas.
Name: GW (aka George Washington)
Species: Hamster
Crimes: Inventor of the Sunflower Seed Slingshot and the Rodent Catapult Transportation Device
But prison can't stop me. I am now building my greatest invention ever...
A
B
the Hairy Houdini Escape-O-Matic.* I just have to locate the final missing piece—and I'll be free!
*patent pending

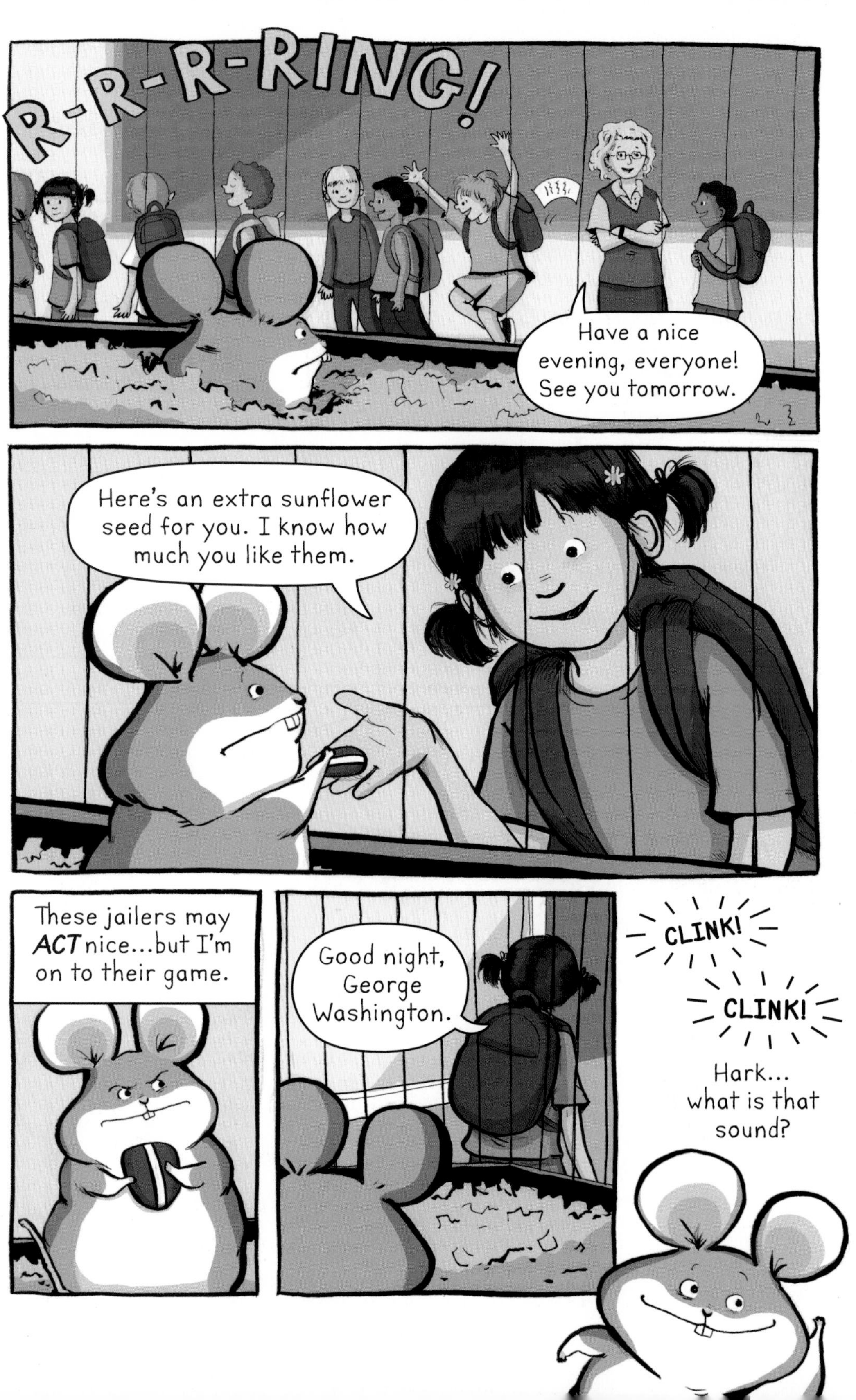
R-R-R-RING!
Have a nice evening, everyone! See you tomorrow.
Here's an extra sunflower seed for you. I know how much you like them.
These jailers may *ACT* nice...but I'm on to their game.
Good night, George Washington.
CLINK!
CLINK!
Hark... what is that sound?

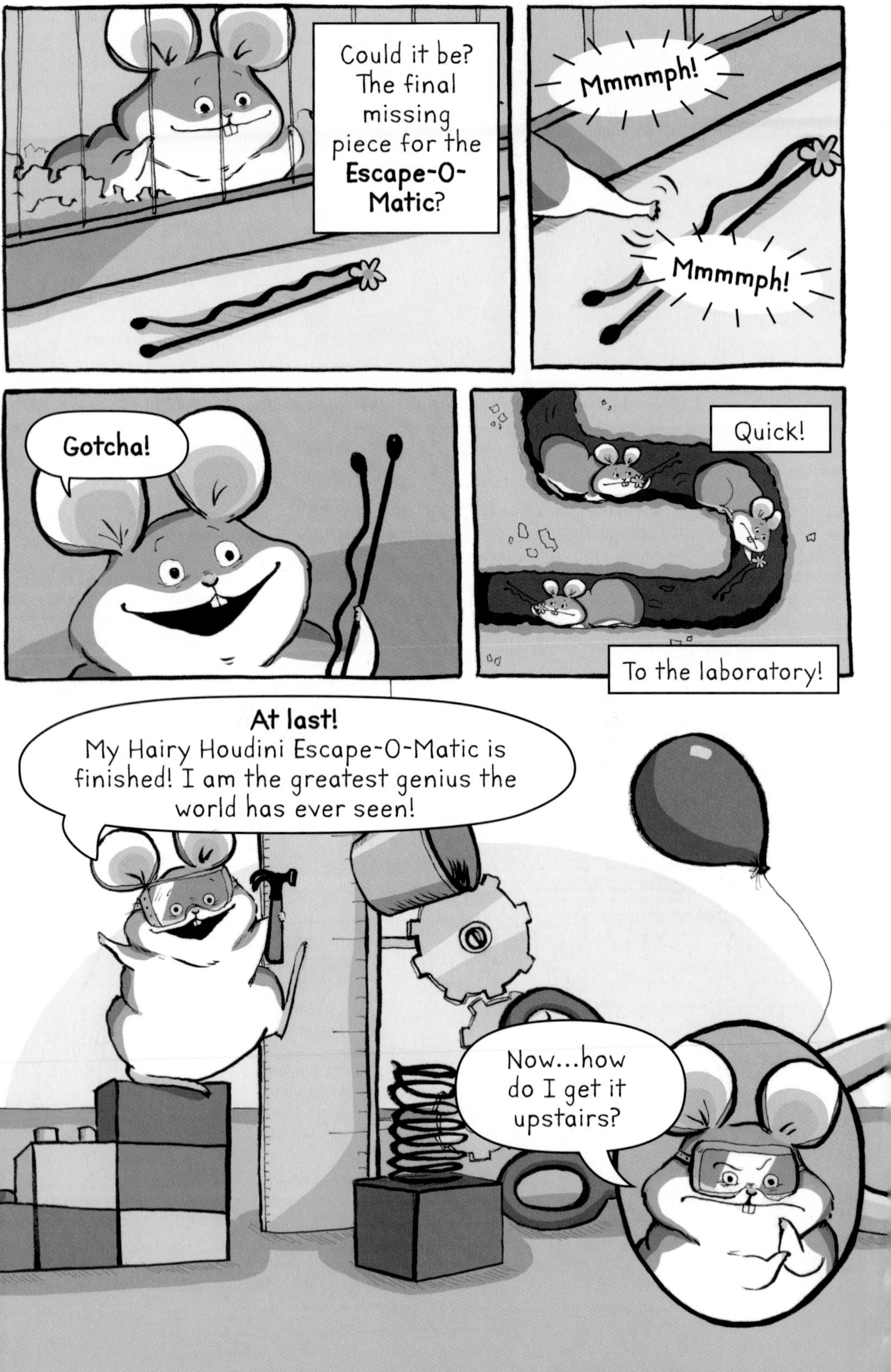
Could it be? The final missing piece for the **Escape-O-Matic**?
Mmmmph!
Mmmmph!
Gotcha!
Quick!
To the laboratory!
At last! My Hairy Houdini Escape-O-Matic is finished! I am the greatest genius the world has ever seen!
Now...how do I get it upstairs?

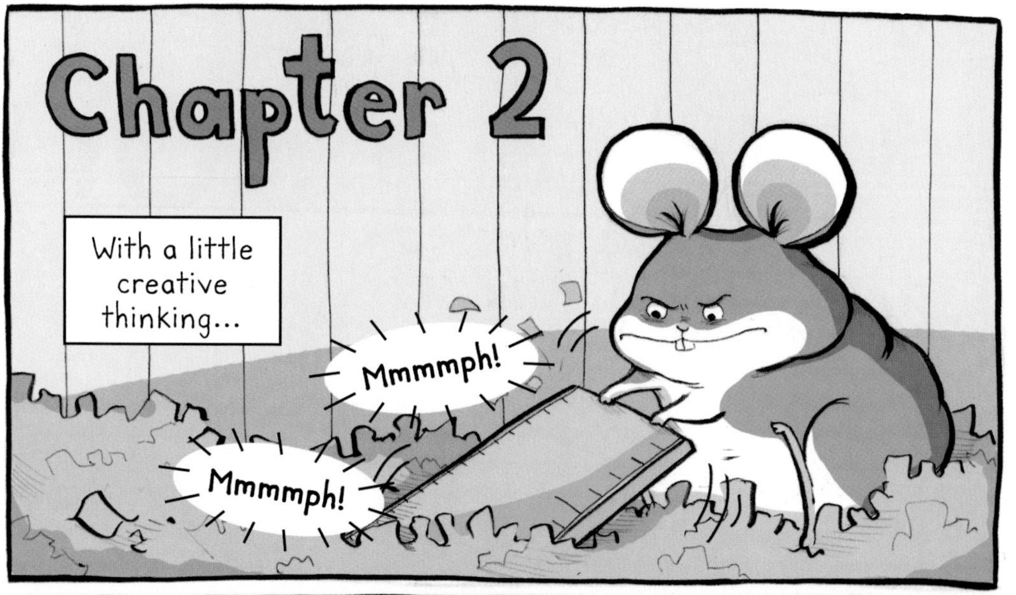
Chapter 2
With a little creative thinking...
Mmmmph!
Mmmmph!

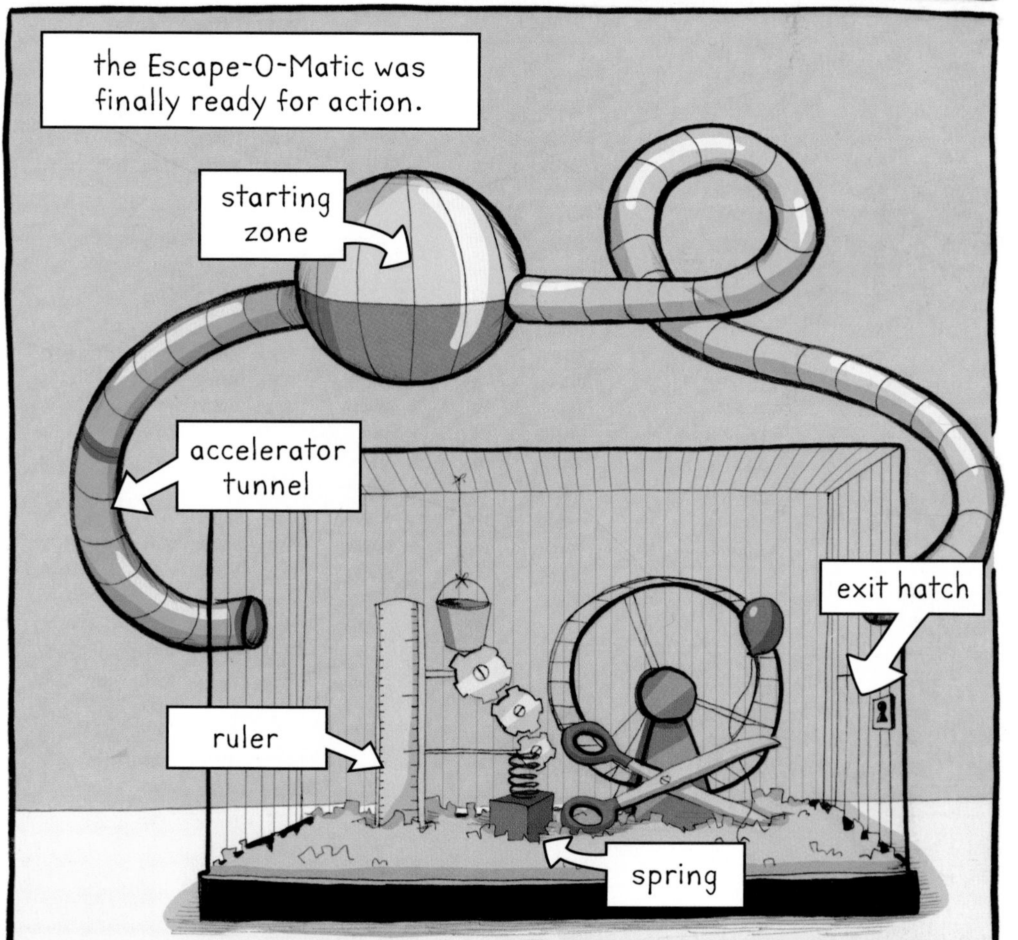
the Escape-O-Matic was finally ready for action.
starting zone
accelerator tunnel
exit hatch
ruler
spring

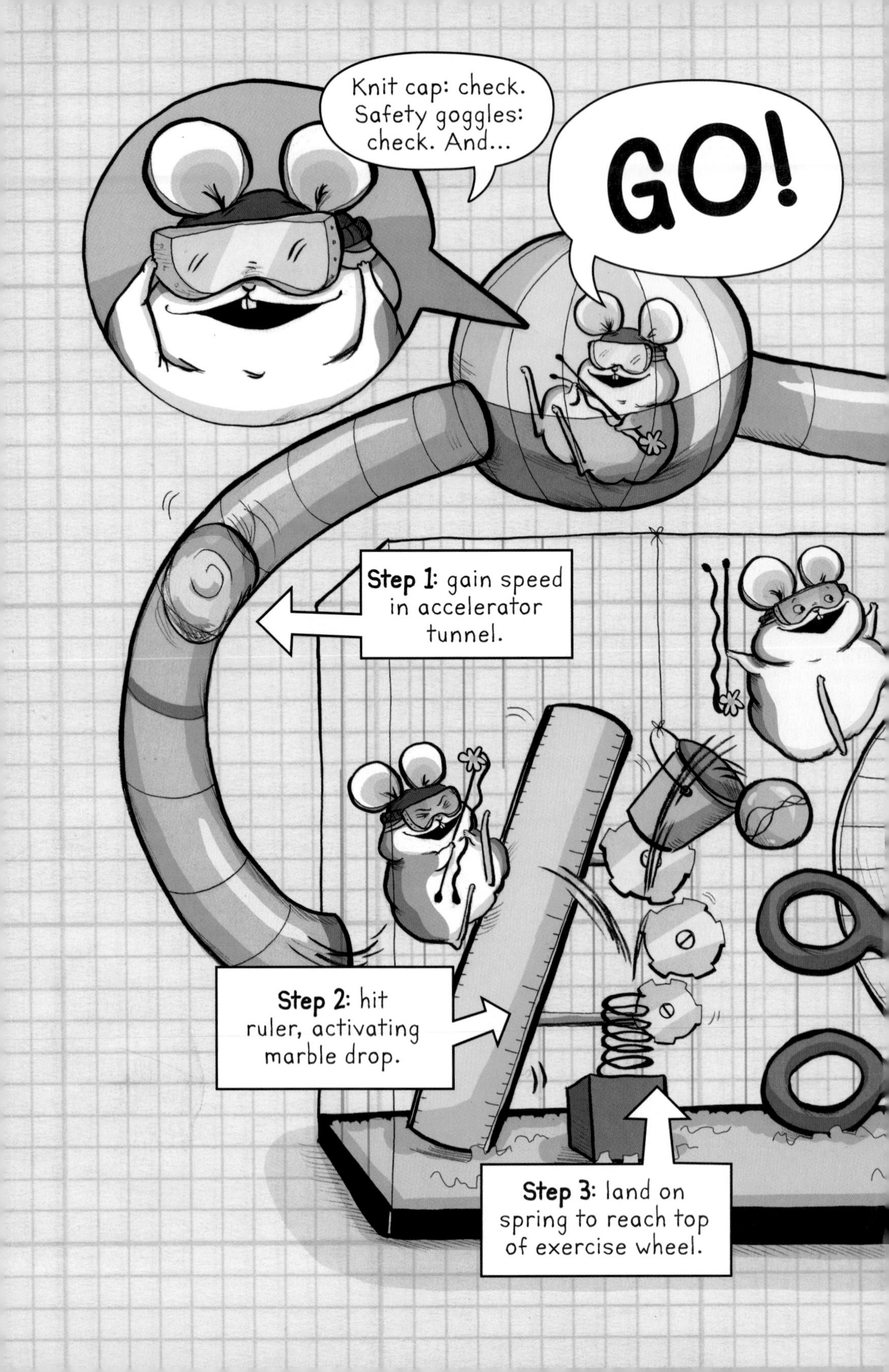

Knit cap: check. Safety goggles: check. And...
GO!
Step 1: gain speed in accelerator tunnel.
Step 2: hit ruler, activating marble drop.
Step 3: land on spring to reach top of exercise wheel.

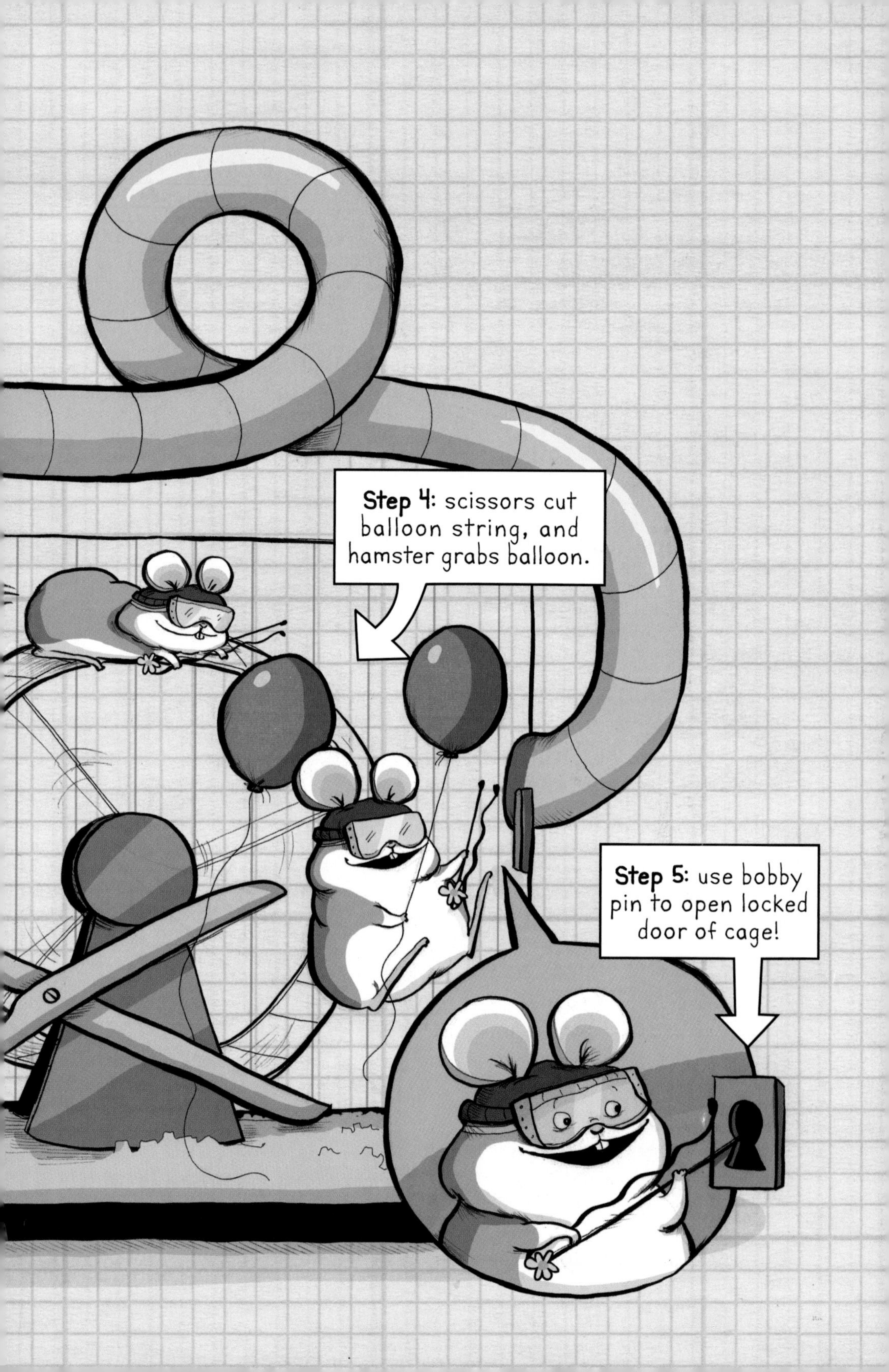
Step 4: scissors cut balloon string, and hamster grabs balloon.
Step 5: use bobby pin to open locked door of cage!

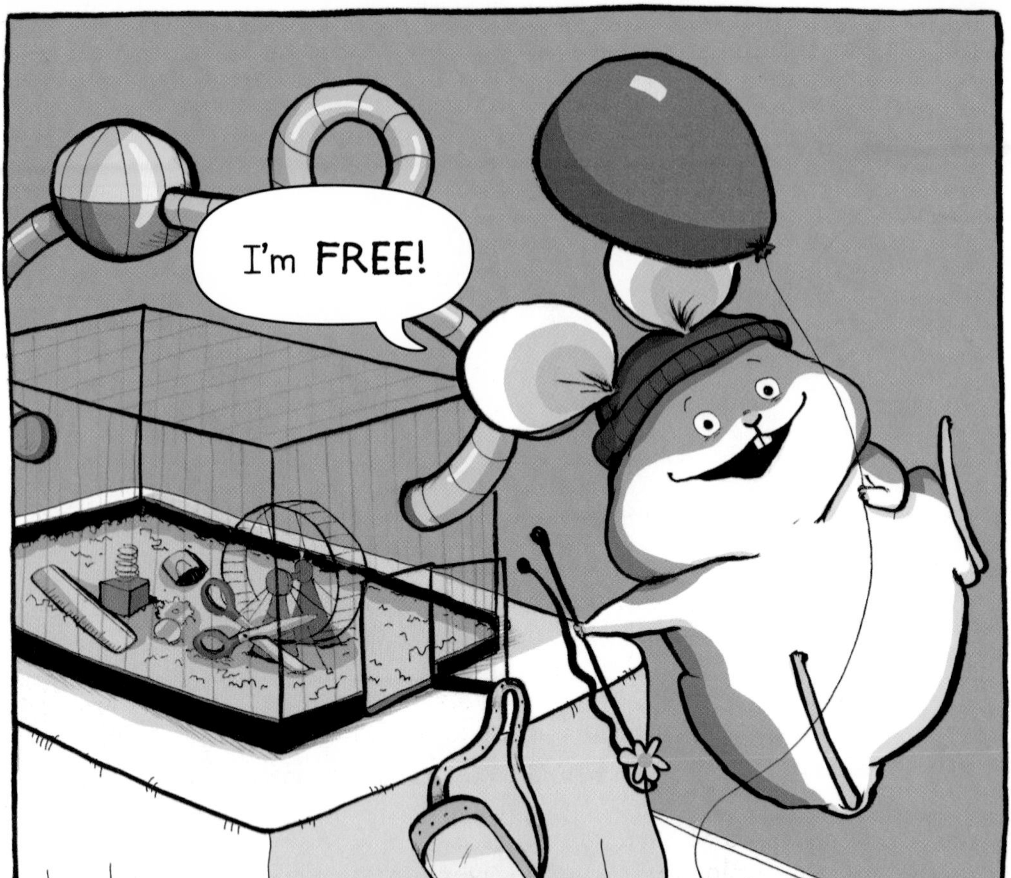
I'm **FREE!**

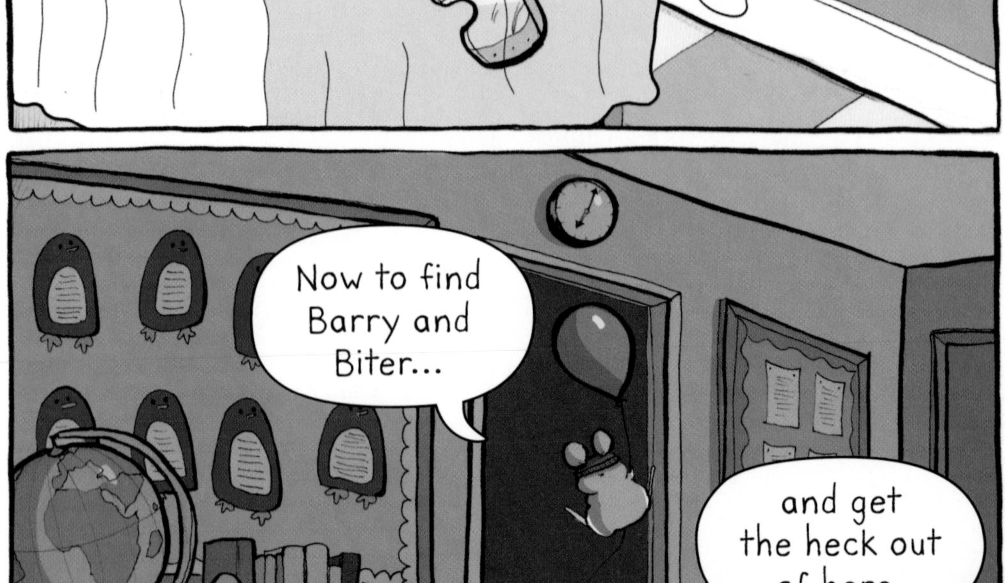
Now to find Barry and Biter...
and get the heck out of here.

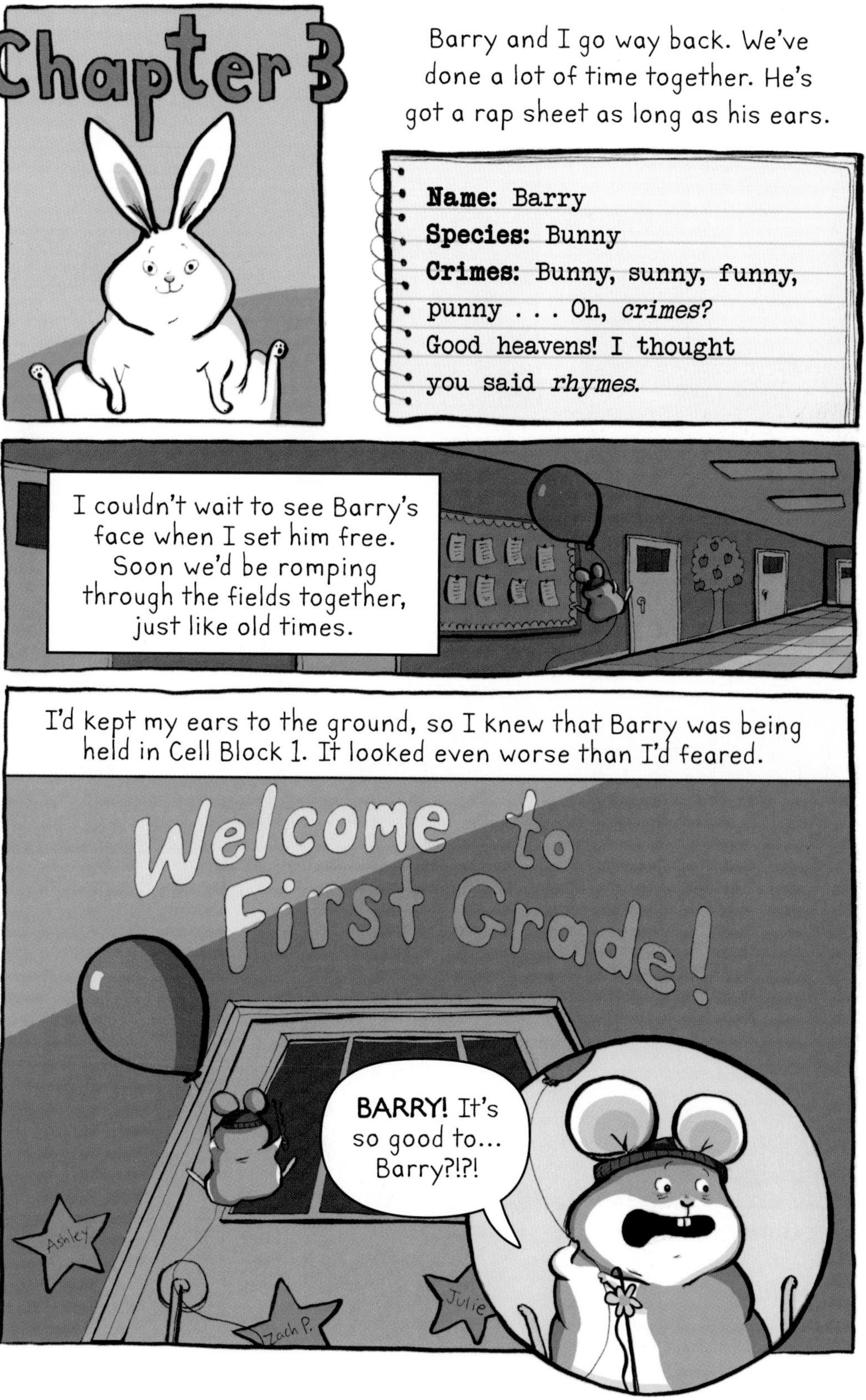
Chapter 3
Barry and I go way back. We've done a lot of time together. He's got a rap sheet as long as his ears.
Name: Barry
Species: Bunny
Crimes: Bunny, sunny, funny, punny . . . Oh, crimes? Good heavens! I thought you said rhymes.
I couldn't wait to see Barry's face when I set him free. Soon we'd be romping through the fields together, just like old times.
I'd kept my ears to the ground, so I knew that Barry was being held in Cell Block 1. It looked even worse than I'd feared.
Welcome to First Grade!
BARRY! It's so good to... Barry?!?!
Ashley
Zach P.
Julie

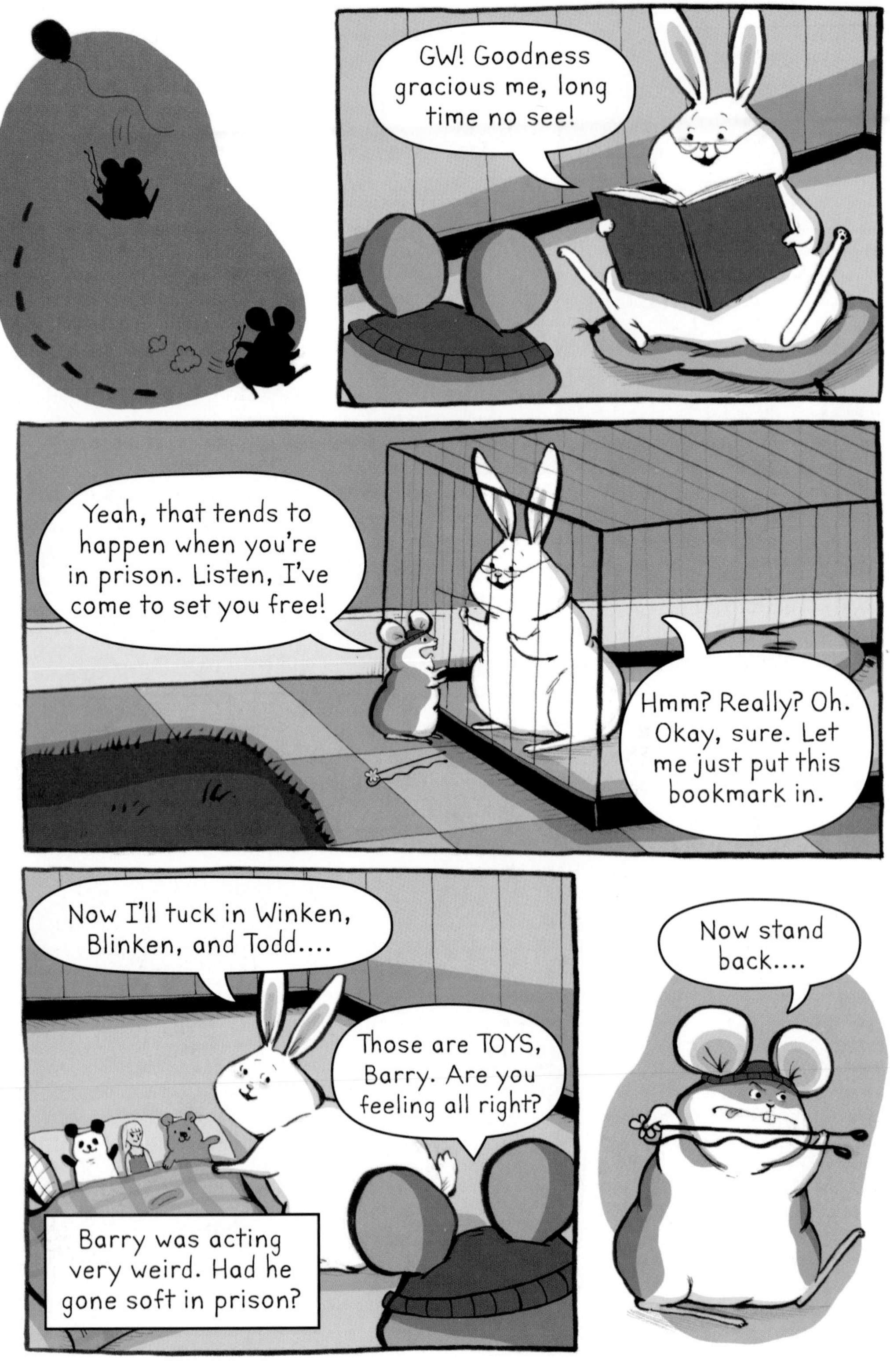
GW! Goodness gracious me, long time no see!
Yeah, that tends to happen when you're in prison. Listen, I've come to set you free!
Hmm? Really? Oh. Okay, sure. Let me just put this bookmark in.
Now I'll tuck in Winken, Blinken, and Todd....
Those are TOYS, Barry. Are you feeling all right?
Barry was acting very weird. Had he gone soft in prison?
Now stand back....

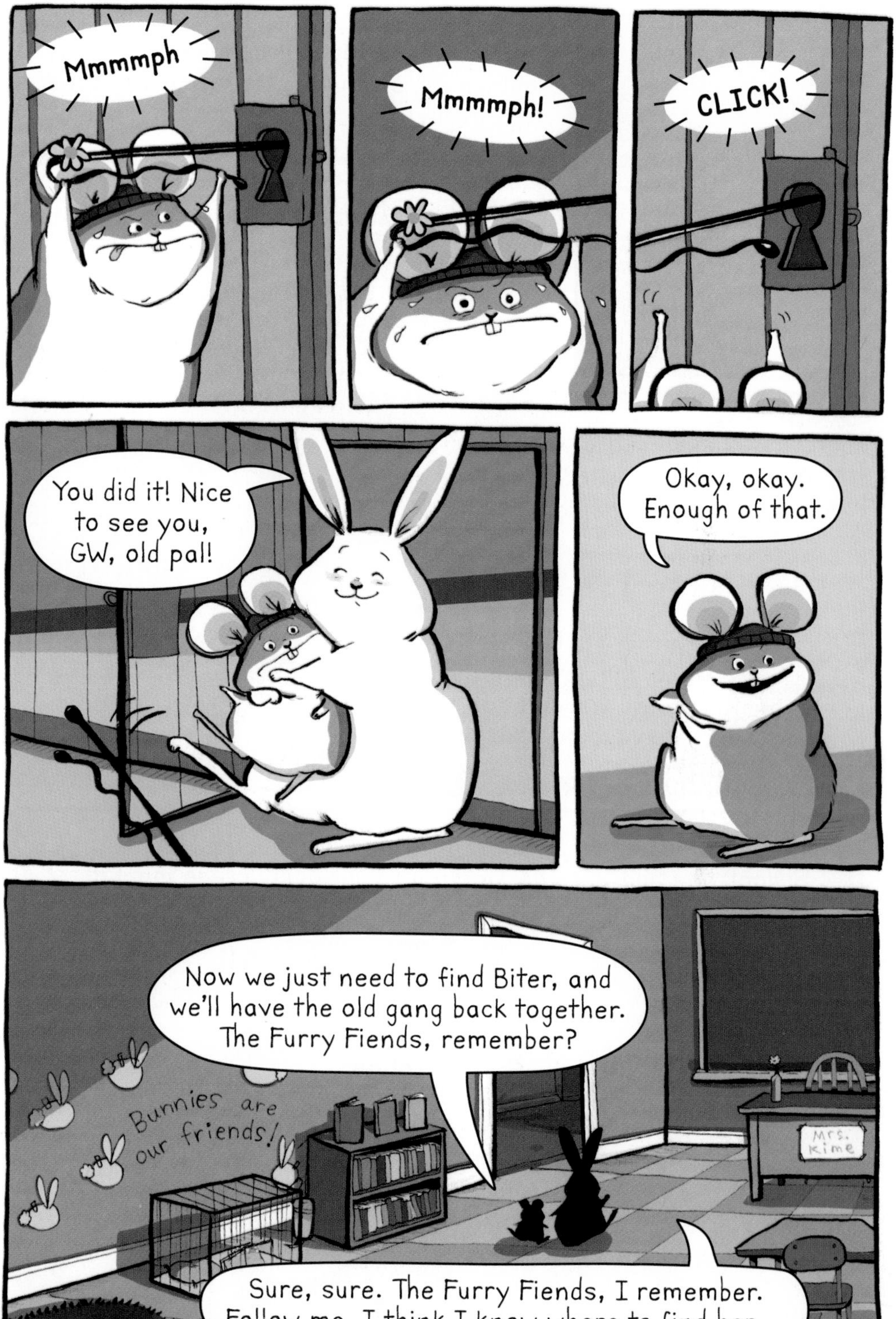
Mmmmph
Mmmmph!
CLICK!
You did it! Nice to see you, GW, old pal!
Okay, okay. Enough of that.
Bunnies are our friends!
Mrs. Kime
Now we just need to find Biter, and we'll have the old gang back together. The Furry Fiends, remember?
Sure, sure. The Furry Fiends, I remember. Follow me. I think I know where to find her....

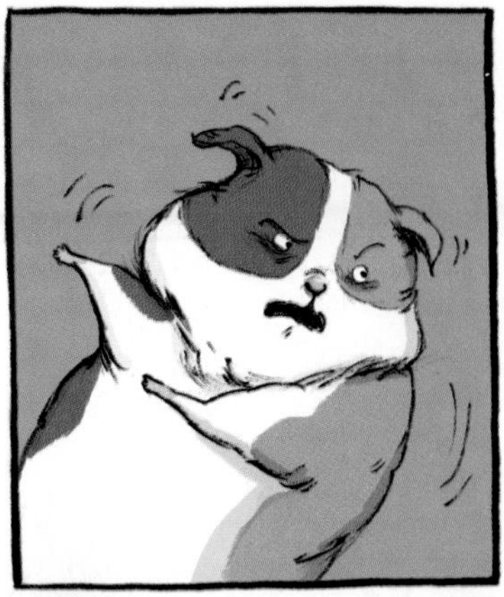

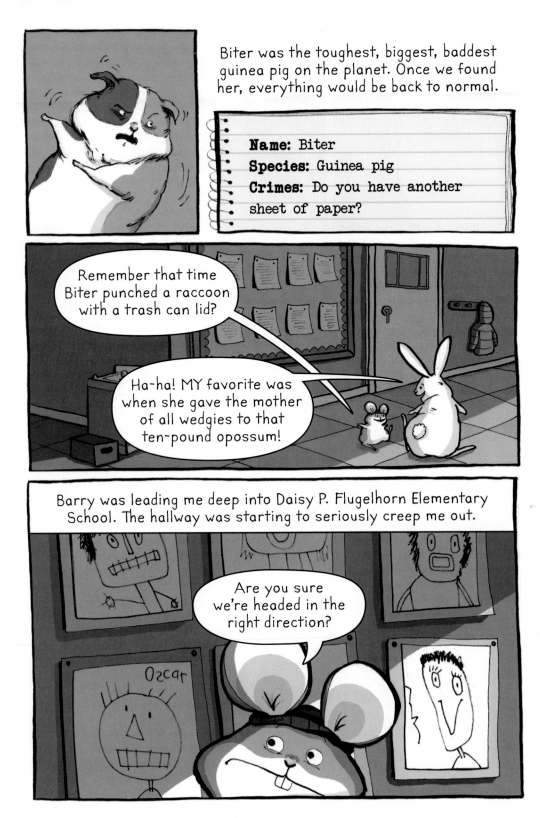

Biter was the toughest, biggest, baddest guinea pig on the planet. Once we found her, everything would be back to normal.

Name: Biter
Species: Guinea pig
Crimes: Do you have another sheet of paper?

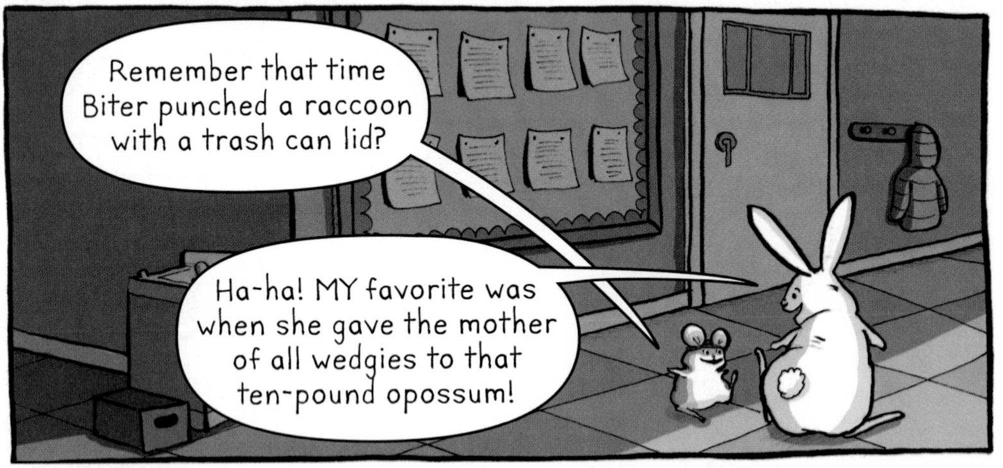

Remember that time Biter punched a raccoon with a trash can lid?
Ha-ha! MY favorite was when she gave the mother of all wedgies to that ten-pound opossum!

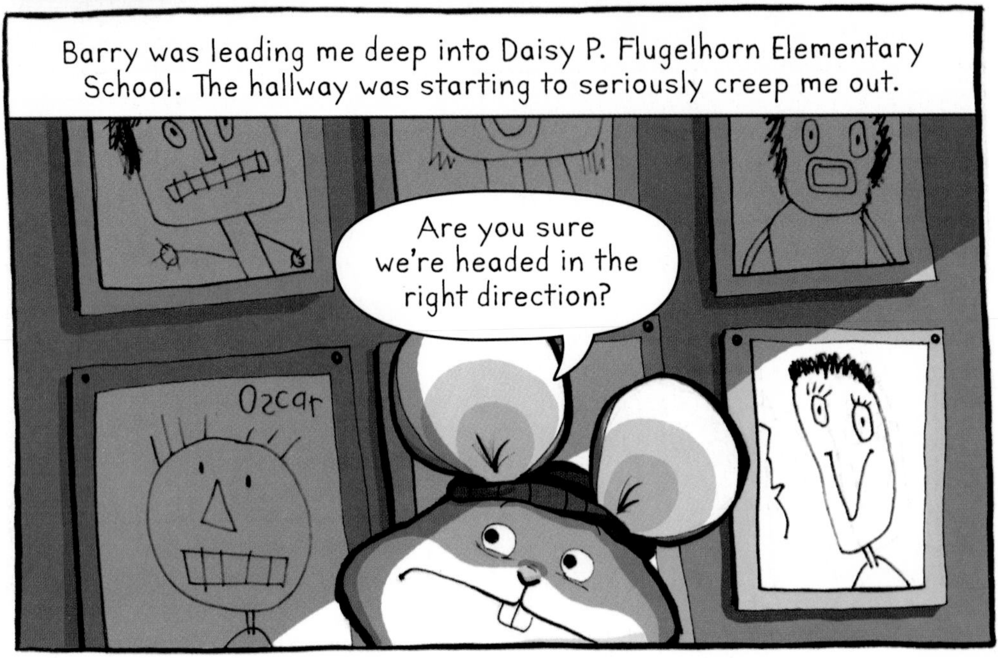

Barry was leading me deep into Daisy P. Flugelhorn Elementary School. The hallway was starting to seriously creep me out.
Are you sure we're headed in the right direction?
Oscar

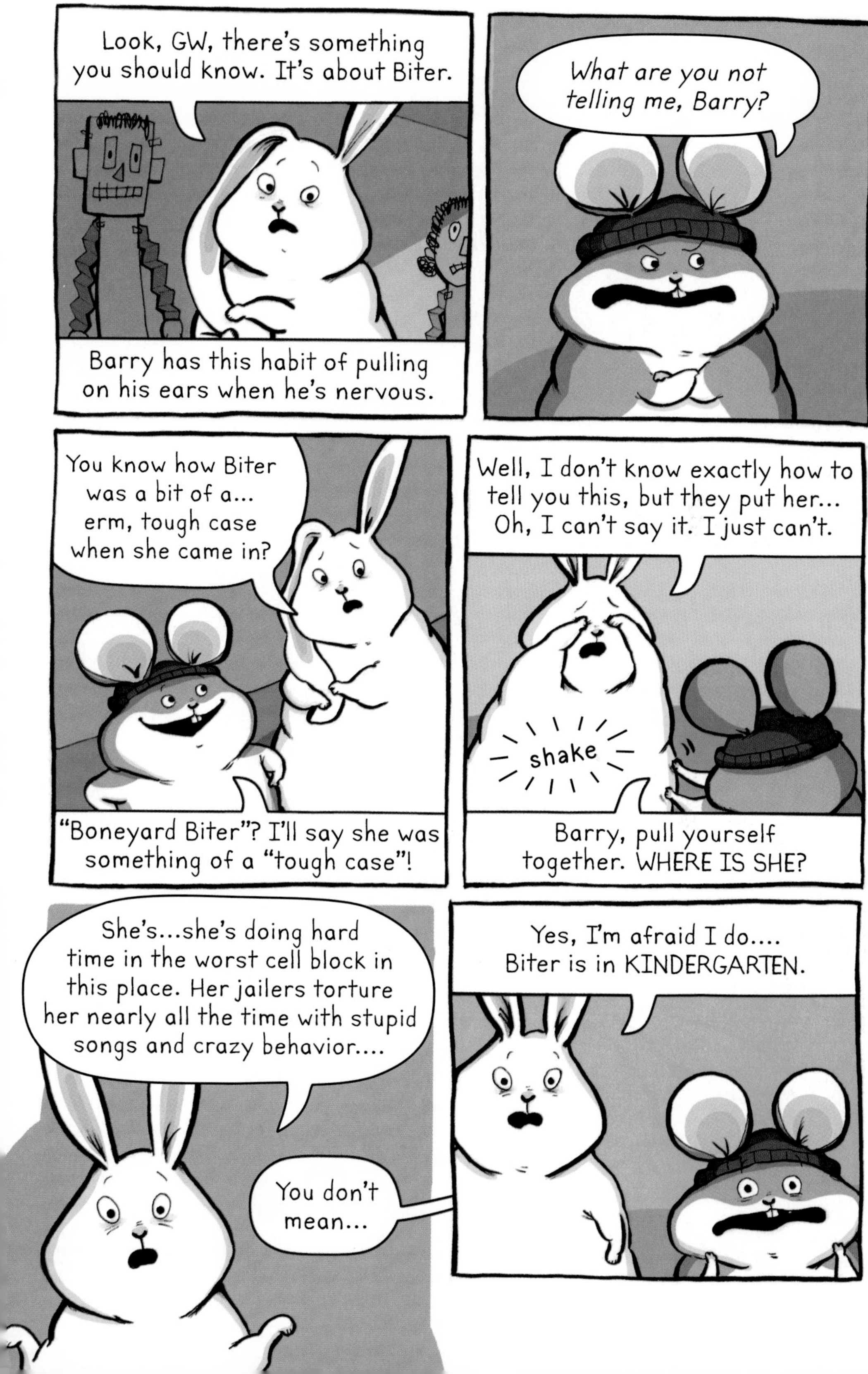

Look, GW, there's something you should know. It's about Biter.
Barry has this habit of pulling on his ears when he's nervous.
What are you not telling me, Barry?
You know how Biter was a bit of a... erm, tough case when she came in?
"Boneyard Biter"? I'll say she was something of a "tough case"!
Well, I don't know exactly how to tell you this, but they put her... Oh, I can't say it. I just can't.
shake
Barry, pull yourself together. WHERE IS SHE?
She's...she's doing hard time in the worst cell block in this place. Her jailers torture her nearly all the time with stupid songs and crazy behavior....
You don't mean...
Yes, I'm afraid I do.... Biter is in KINDERGARTEN.

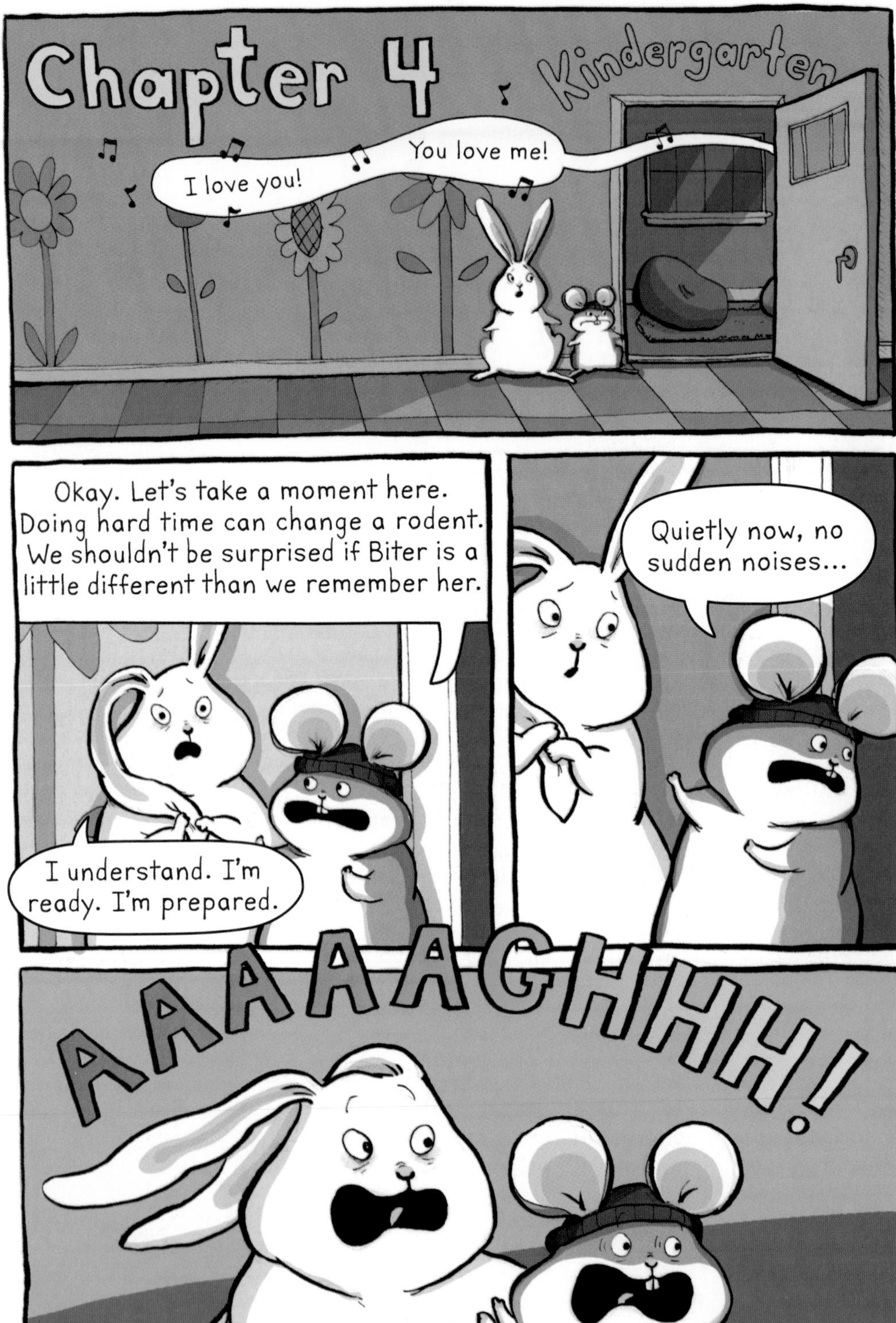
Chapter 4
Kindergarten
I love you!
You love me!
Okay. Let's take a moment here. Doing hard time can change a rodent. We shouldn't be surprised if Biter is a little different than we remember her.
I understand. I'm ready. I'm prepared.
Quietly now, no sudden noises...
AAAAAGHHHH!

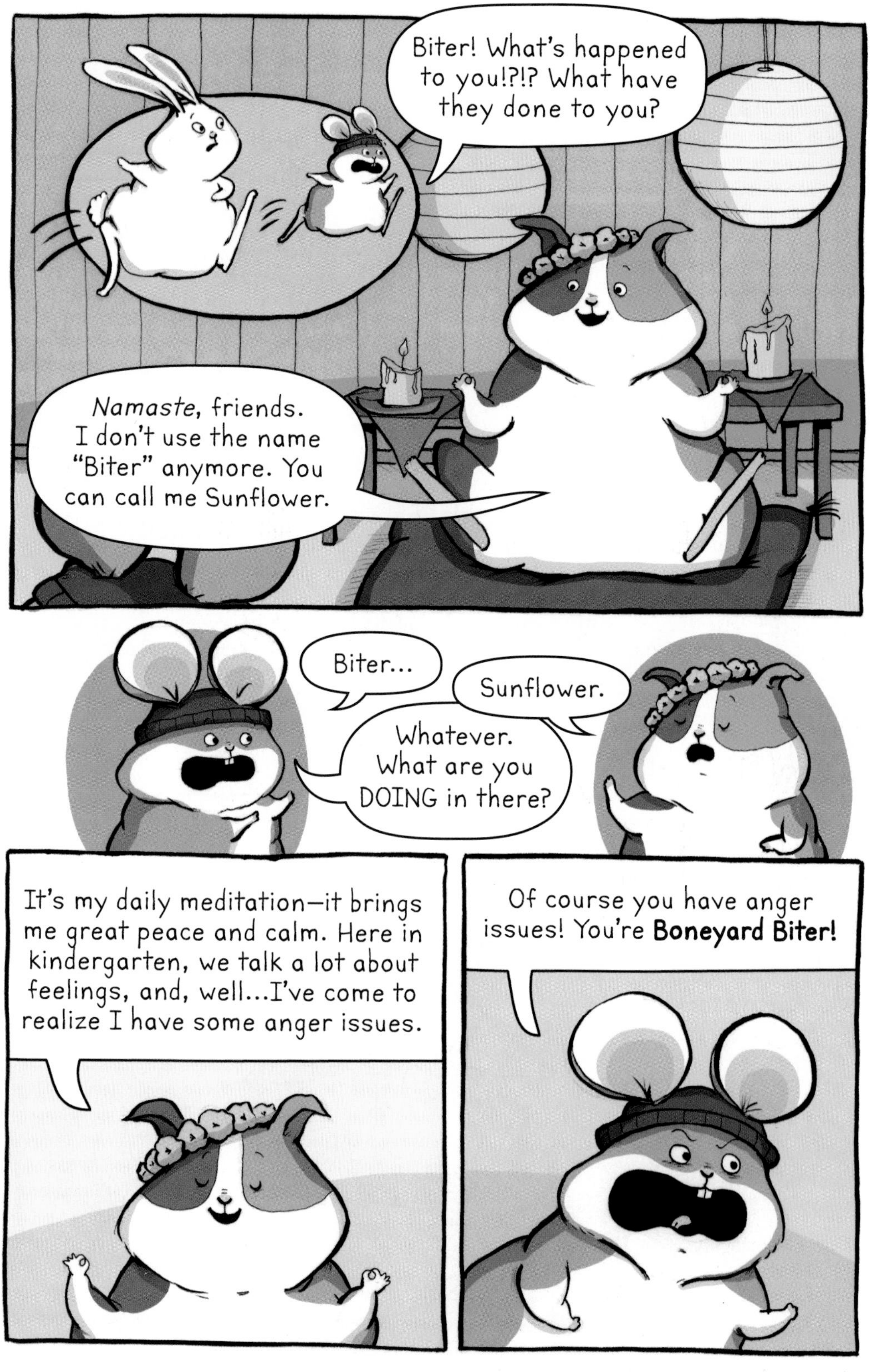

Biter! What's happened to you!?!? What have they done to you?
Namaste, friends. I don't use the name "Biter" anymore. You can call me Sunflower.
Biter...
Sunflower.
Whatever. What are you DOING in there?
It's my daily meditation—it brings me great peace and calm. Here in kindergarten, we talk a lot about feelings, and, well...I've come to realize I have some anger issues.
Of course you have anger issues! You're **Boneyard Biter!**

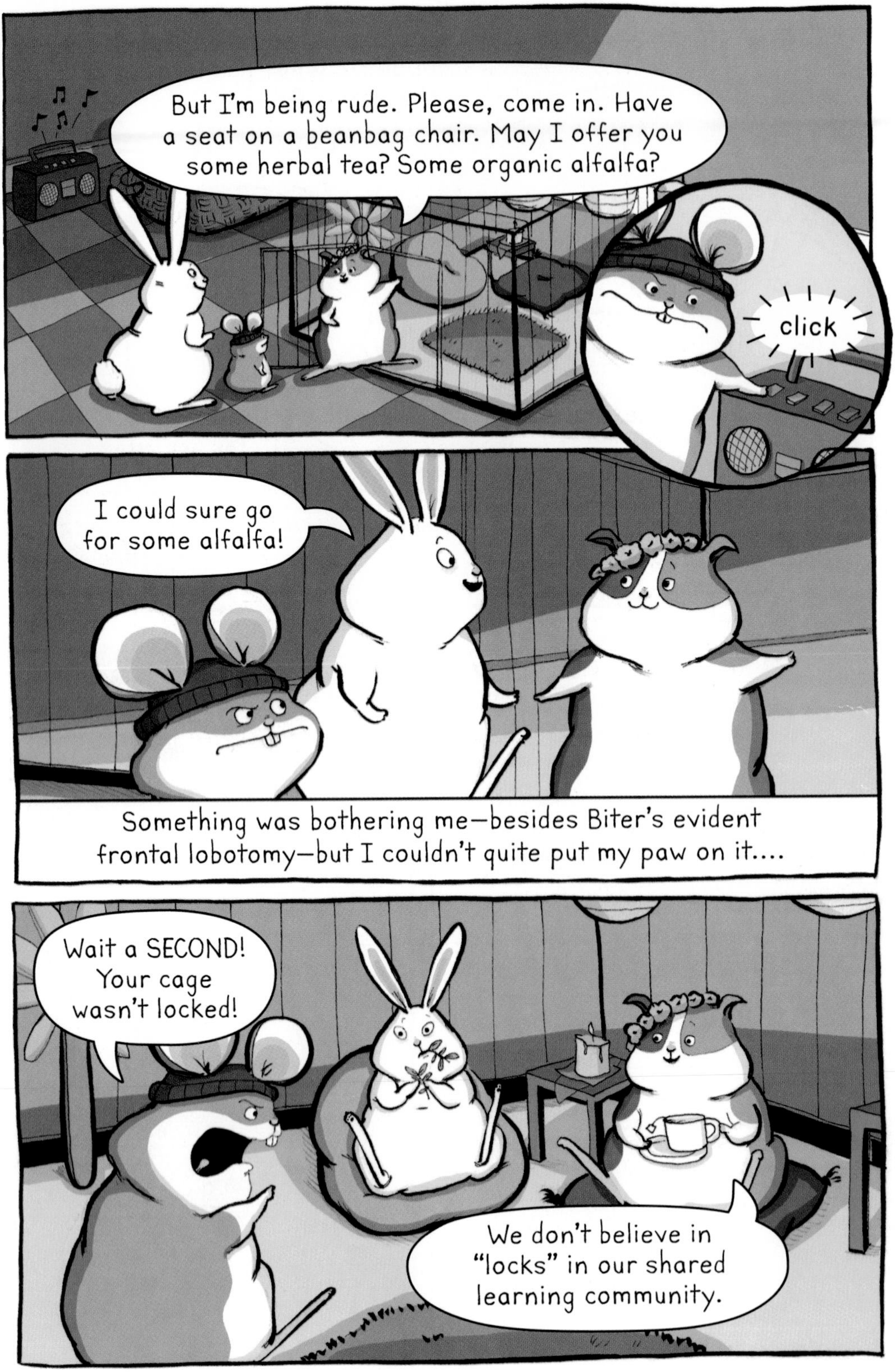
But I'm being rude. Please, come in. Have a seat on a beanbag chair. May I offer you some herbal tea? Some organic alfalfa?
click
I could sure go for some alfalfa!
Something was bothering me—besides Biter's evident frontal lobotomy—but I couldn't quite put my paw on it....
Wait a SECOND! Your cage wasn't locked!
We don't believe in "locks" in our shared learning community.

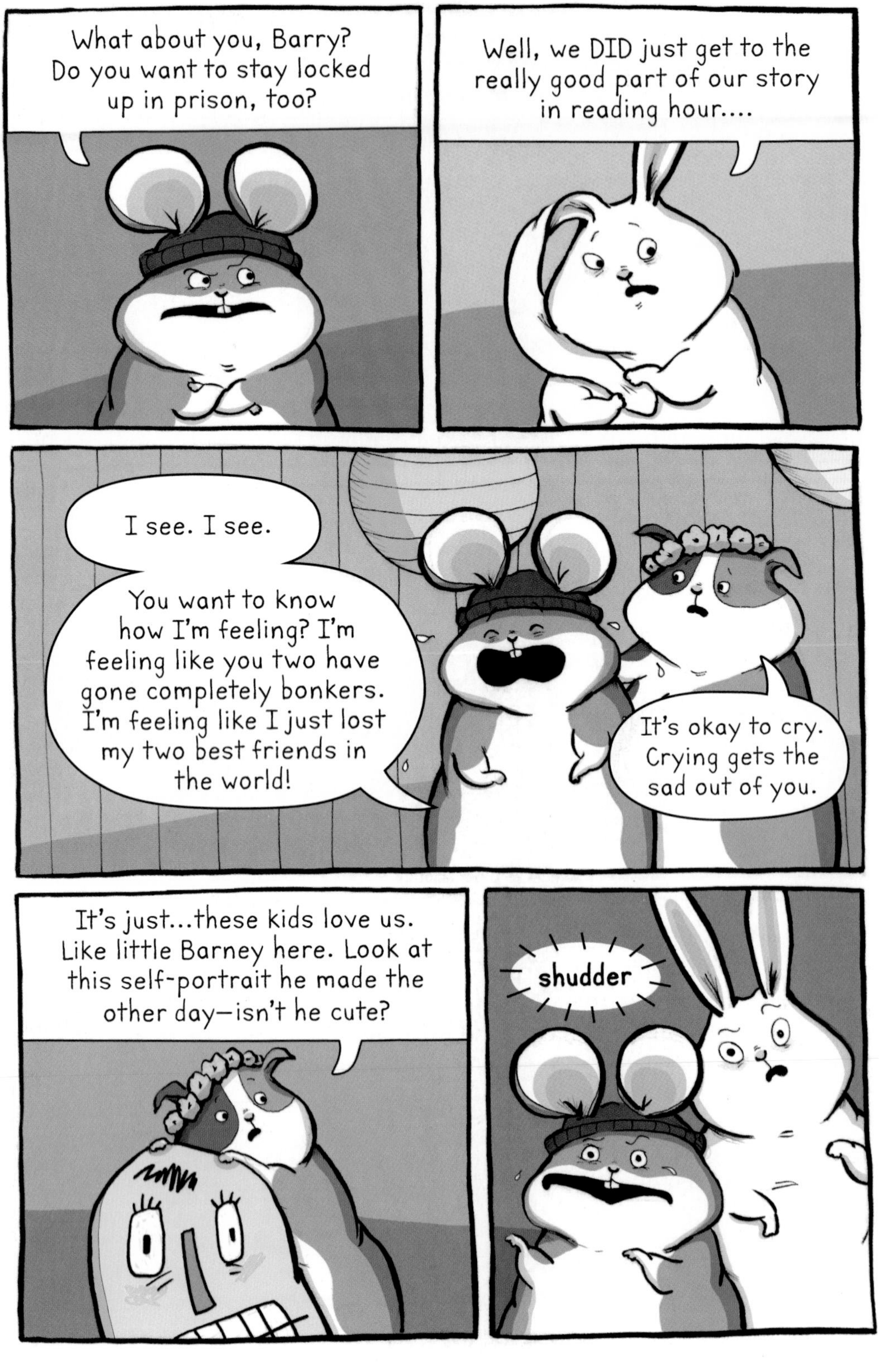
What about you, Barry? Do you want to stay locked up in prison, too?
Well, we DID just get to the really good part of our story in reading hour....
I see. I see.
You want to know how I'm feeling? I'm feeling like you two have gone completely bonkers. I'm feeling like I just lost my two best friends in the world!
It's okay to cry. Crying gets the sad out of you.
It's just...these kids love us. Like little Barney here. Look at this self-portrait he made the other day—isn't he cute?
shudder

23

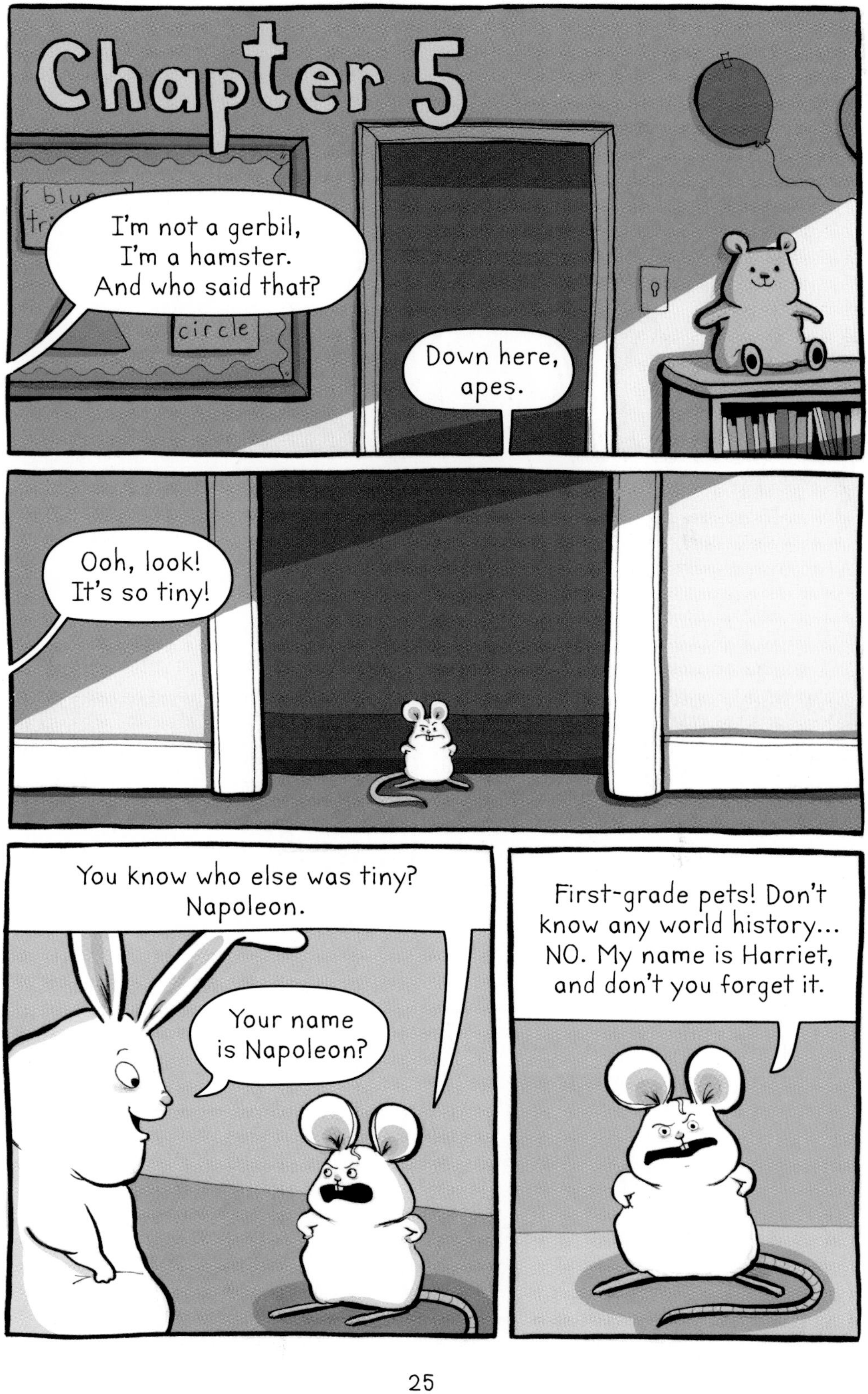
Chapter 5
I'm not a gerbil, I'm a hamster. And who said that?
circle
Down here, apes.
Ooh, look! It's so tiny!
You know who else was tiny? Napoleon.
Your name is Napoleon?
First-grade pets! Don't know any world history... NO. My name is Harriet, and don't you forget it.

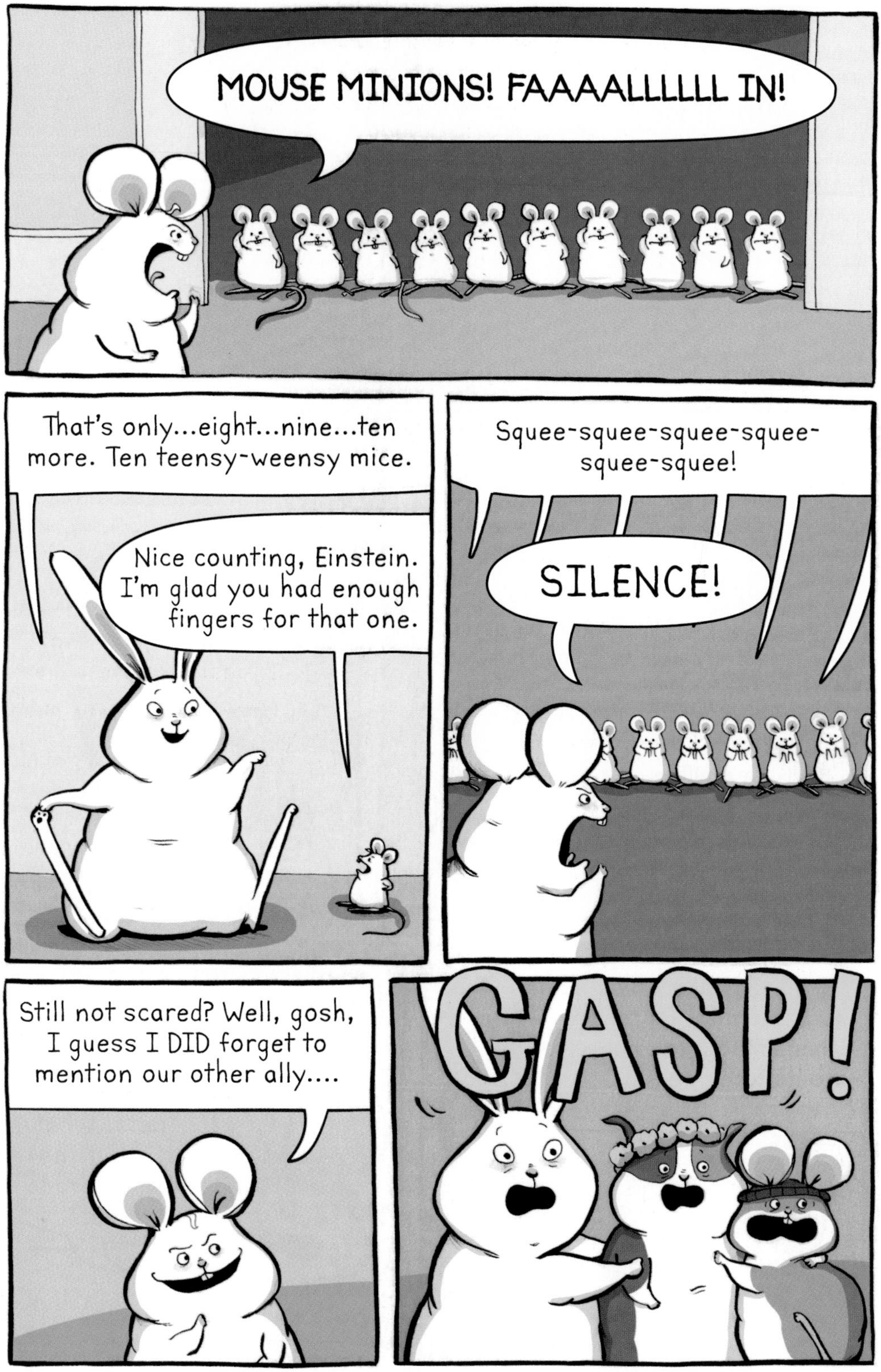
MOUSE MINIONS! FAAAALLLLLL IN!
That's only...eight...nine...ten more. Ten teensy-weensy mice.
Nice counting, Einstein. I'm glad you had enough fingers for that one.
Squee-squee-squee-squee-squee-squee!
SILENCE!
Still not scared? Well, gosh, I guess I DID forget to mention our other ally....
GASP!

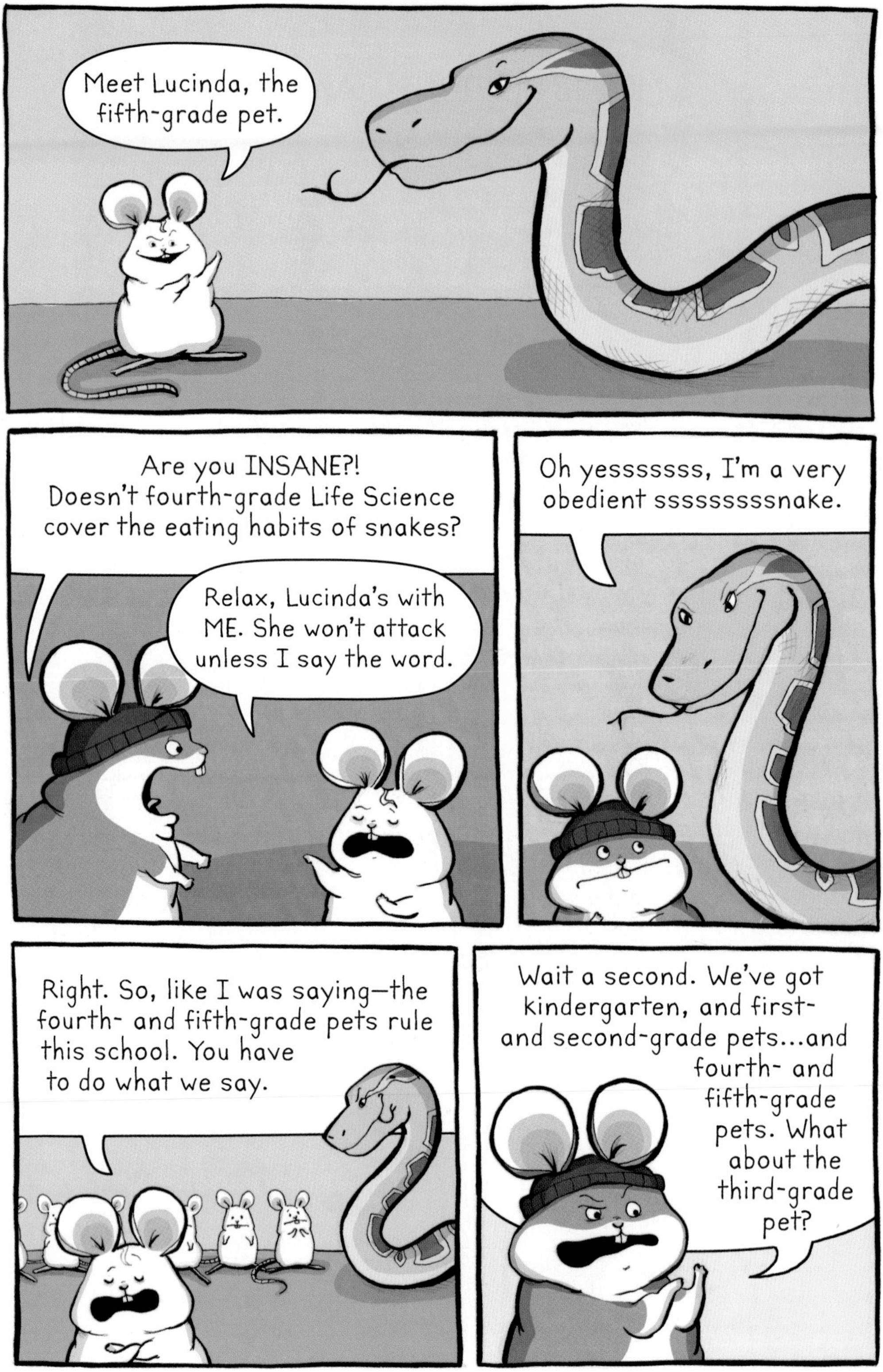
Meet Lucinda, the fifth-grade pet.
Are you INSANE?! Doesn't fourth-grade Life Science cover the eating habits of snakes?
Relax, Lucinda's with ME. She won't attack unless I say the word.
Oh yesssssss, I'm a very obedient sssssssssnake.
Right. So, like I was saying—the fourth- and fifth-grade pets rule this school. You have to do what we say.
Wait a second. We've got kindergarten, and first- and second-grade pets...and fourth- and fifth-grade pets. What about the third-grade pet?

29

31

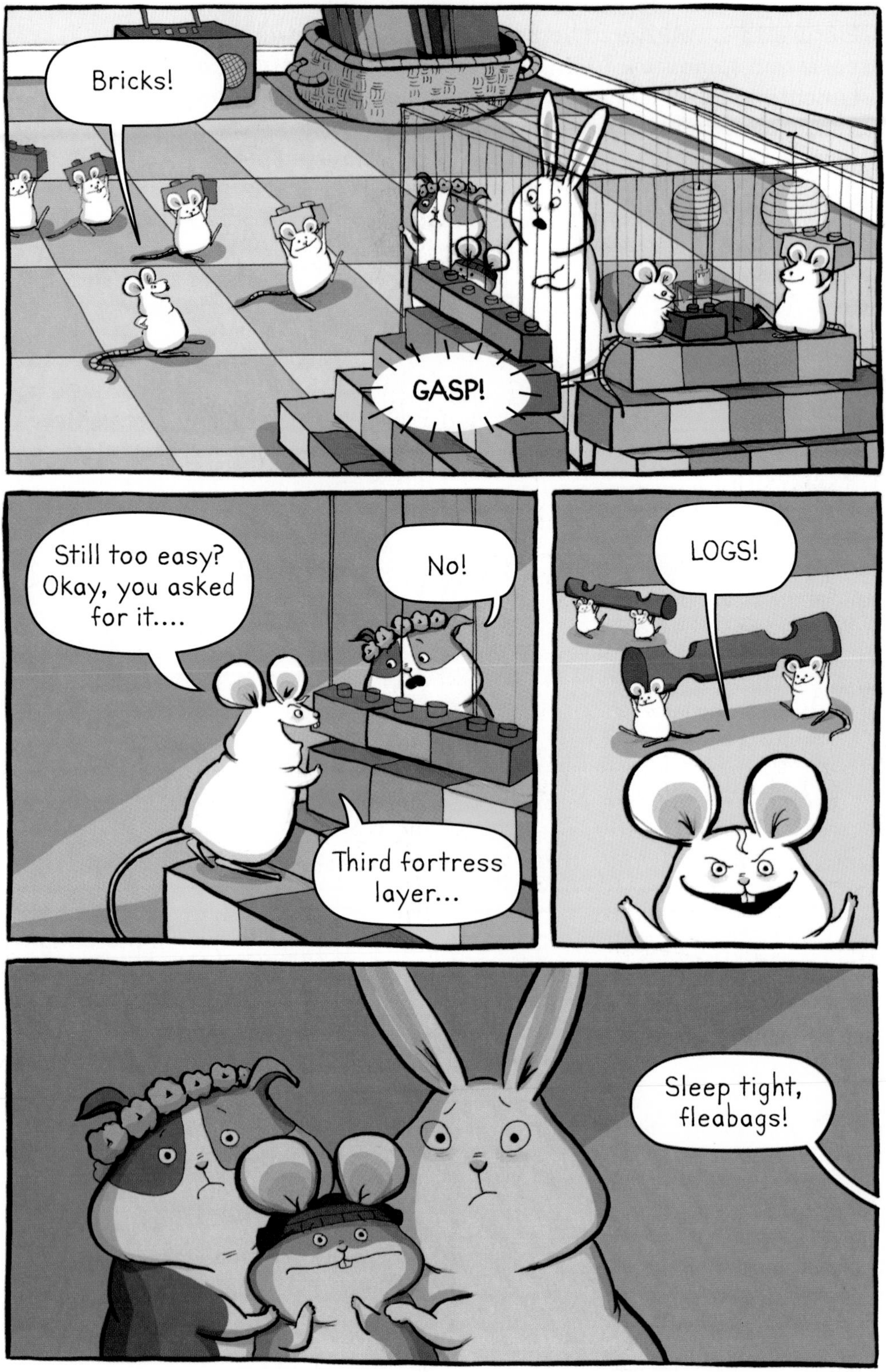
Bricks!
GASP!
Still too easy? Okay, you asked for it....
No!
Third fortress layer...
LOGS!
Sleep tight, fleabags!

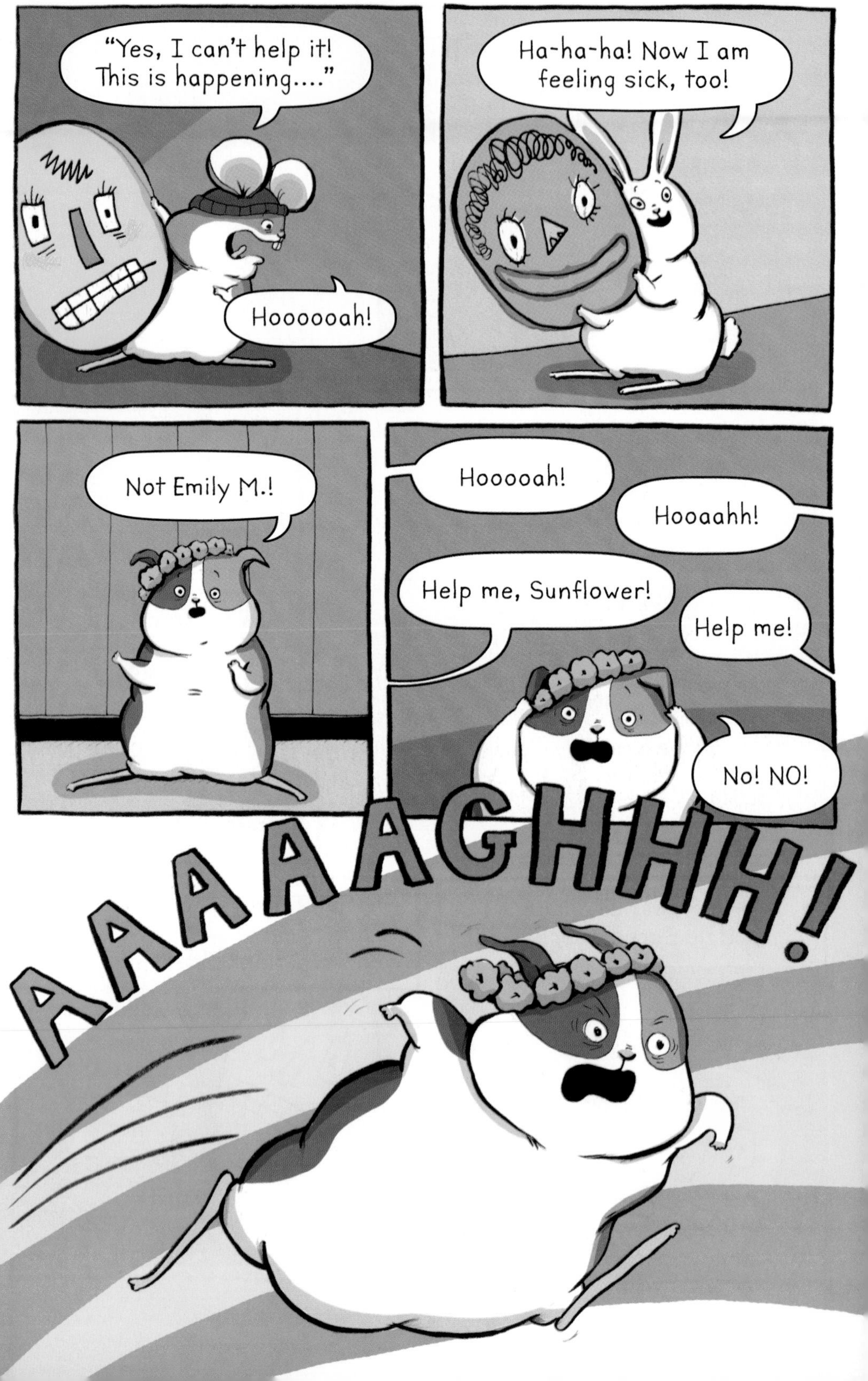
"Yes, I can't help it! This is happening...."
Hooooooah!
Ha-ha-ha! Now I am feeling sick, too!
Not Emily M.!
Hooooah!
Hooaahh!
Help me, Sunflower!
Help me!
No! NO!
AAAAAGHHHH!

Chapter 6

CRASH!

Let's go get those lousy, stinking, rotten mice!

Erm, and ask them very nicely to please stop with their evil plan.

Harriet has a big head start on us. What's the fastest way to get to the cafeteria?

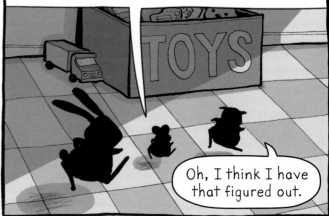

Oh, I think I have that figured out.

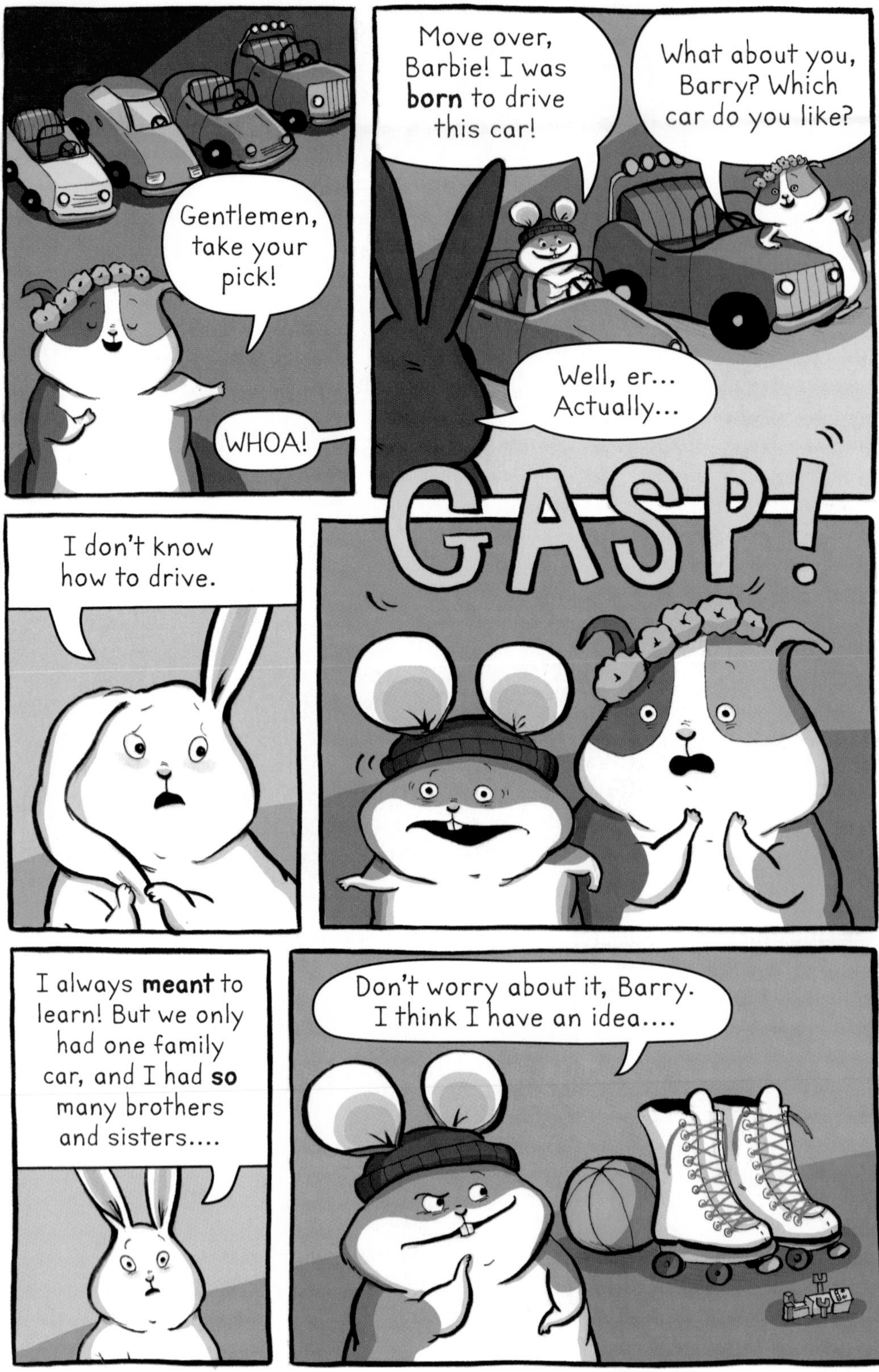
Gentlemen, take your pick!
WHOA!
Move over, Barbie! I was **born** to drive this car!
What about you, Barry? Which car do you like?
Well, er... Actually...
GASP!
I don't know how to drive.
I always **meant** to learn! But we only had one family car, and I had **so** many brothers and sisters....
Don't worry about it, Barry. I think I have an idea....

39

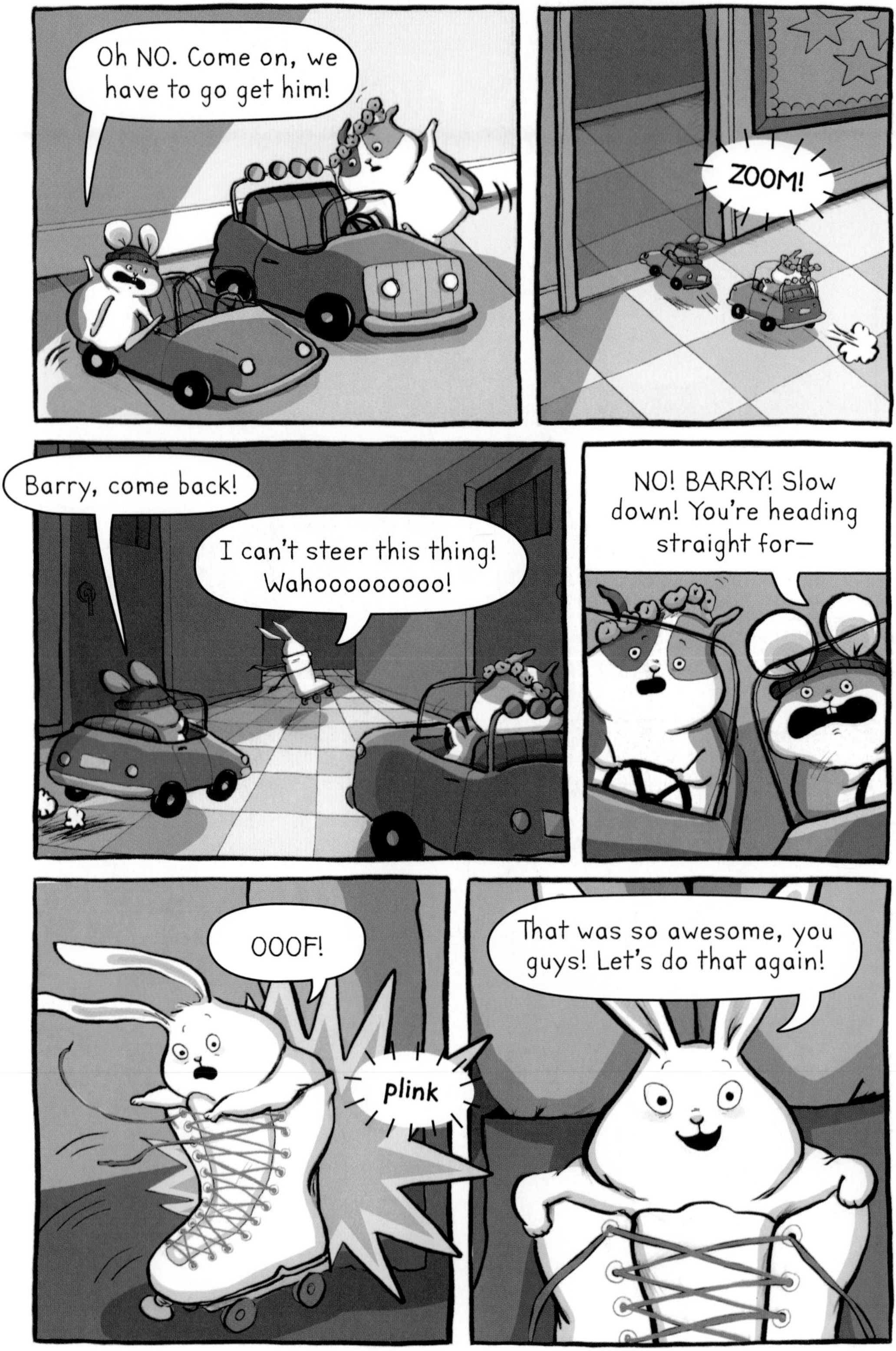
Oh NO. Come on, we have to go get him!
ZOOM!
Barry, come back!
I can't steer this thing! Wahooooooooo!
NO! BARRY! Slow down! You're heading straight for—
OOOF!
plink
That was so awesome, you guys! Let's do that again!

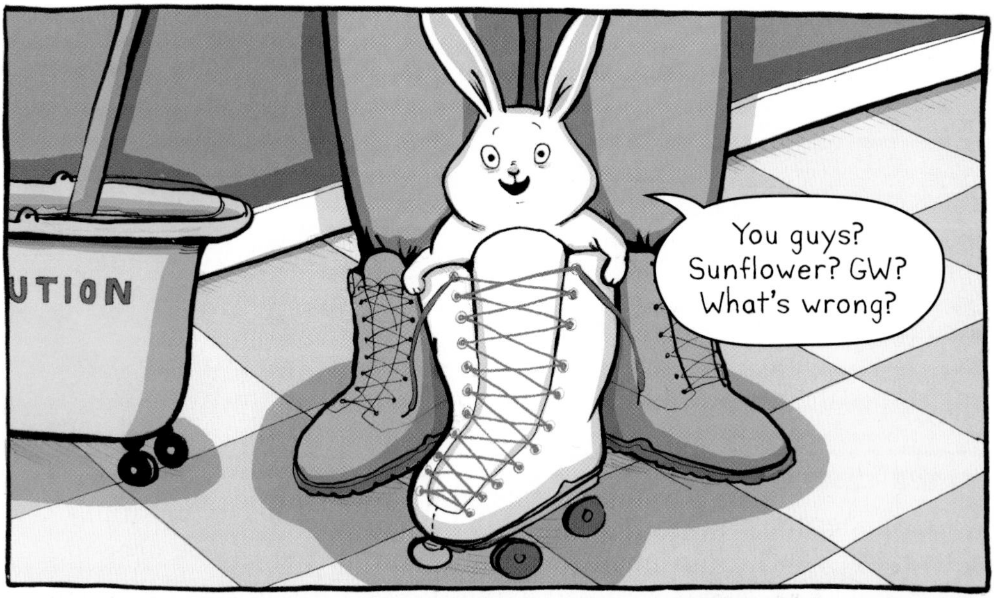
UTION
You guys? Sunflower? GW? What's wrong?

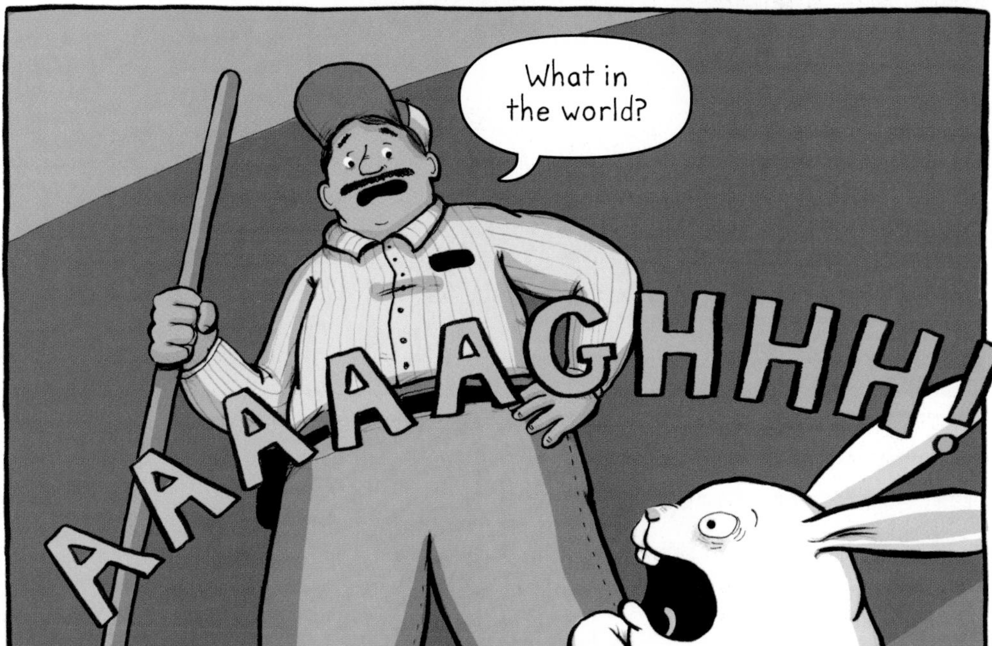
What in the world?
AAAAAGHHH!
ON

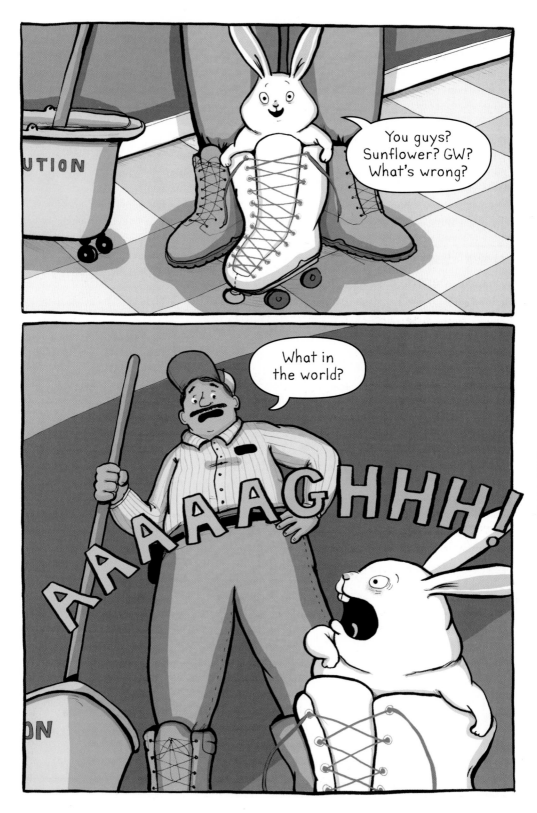

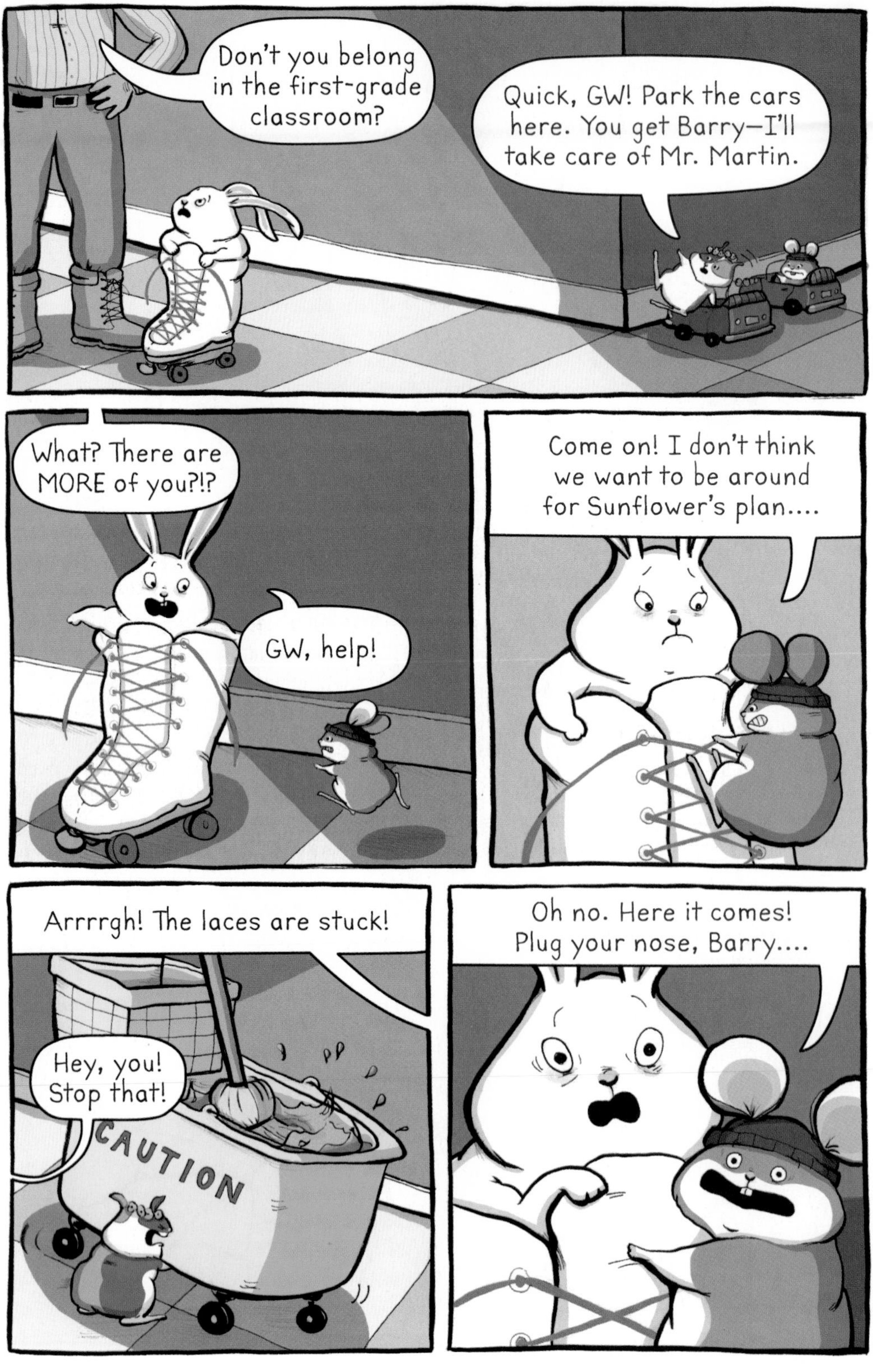
Don't you belong in the first-grade classroom?
Quick, GW! Park the cars here. You get Barry—I'll take care of Mr. Martin.
What? There are MORE of you?!?
GW, help!
Come on! I don't think we want to be around for Sunflower's plan....
Arrrrgh! The laces are stuck!
Hey, you! Stop that!
CAUTION
Oh no. Here it comes! Plug your nose, Barry....

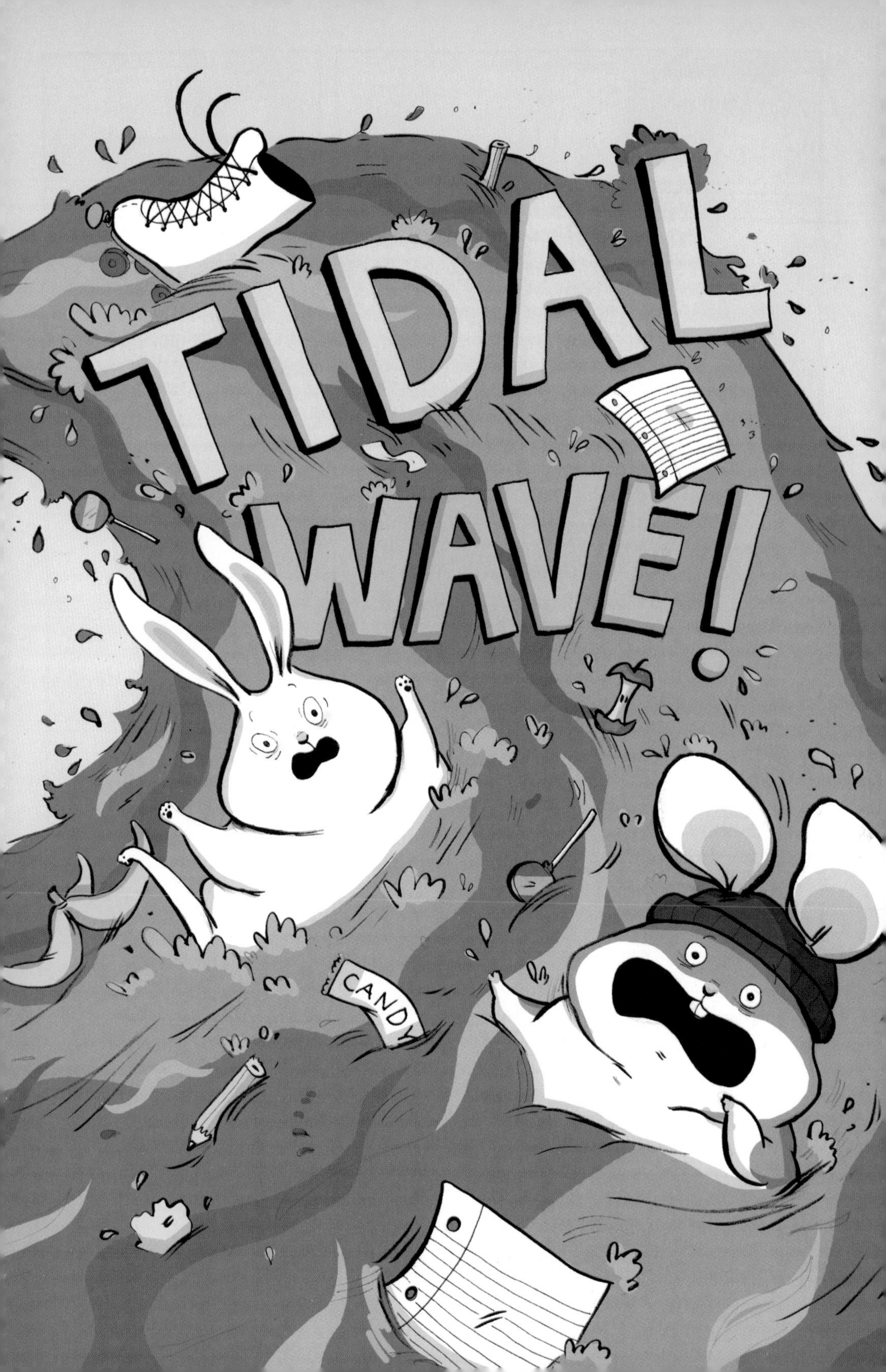
TIDAL WAVE!
CANDY

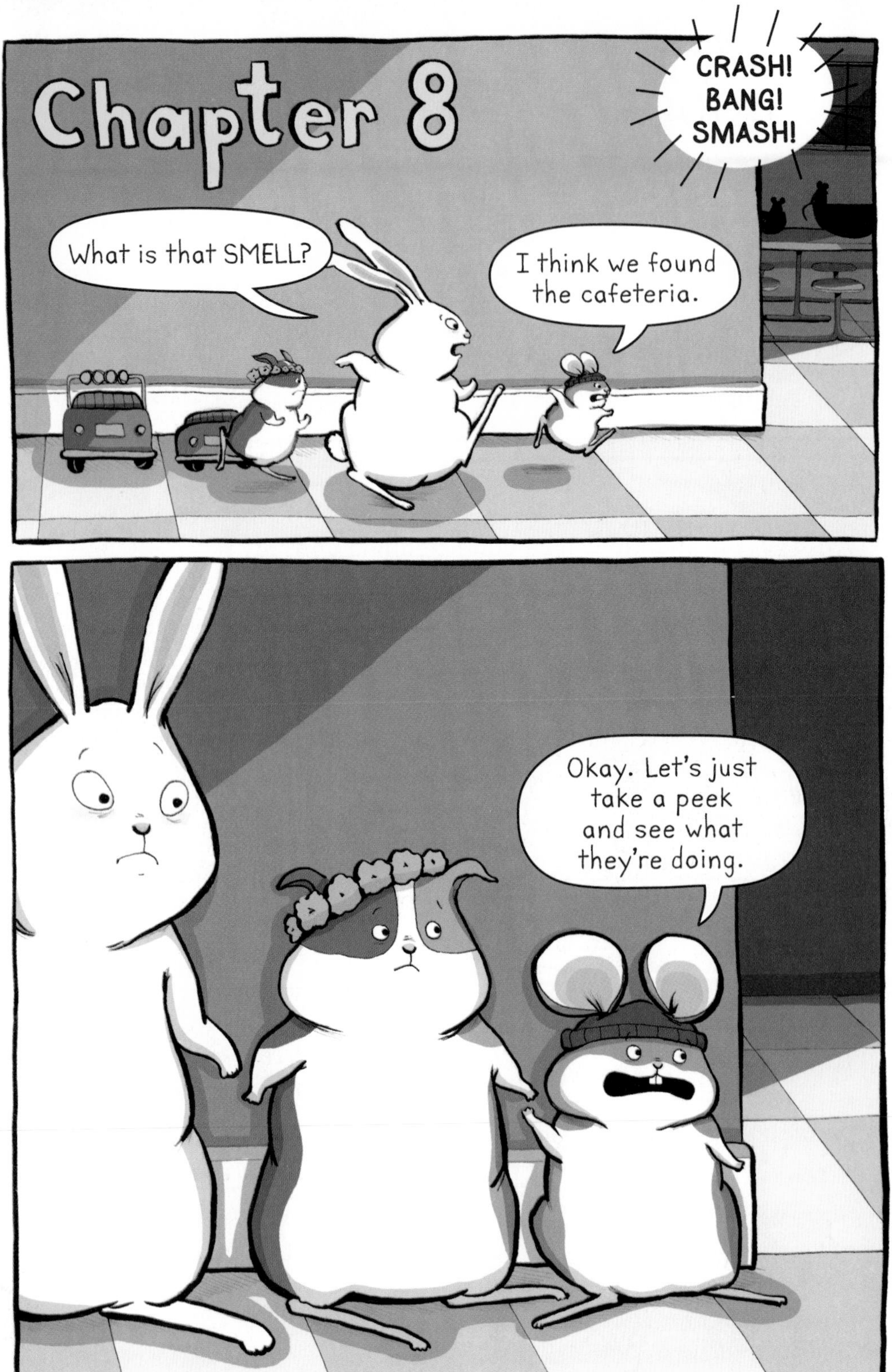
Chapter 8
CRASH! BANG! SMASH!
What is that SMELL?
I think we found the cafeteria.
Okay. Let's just take a peek and see what they're doing.

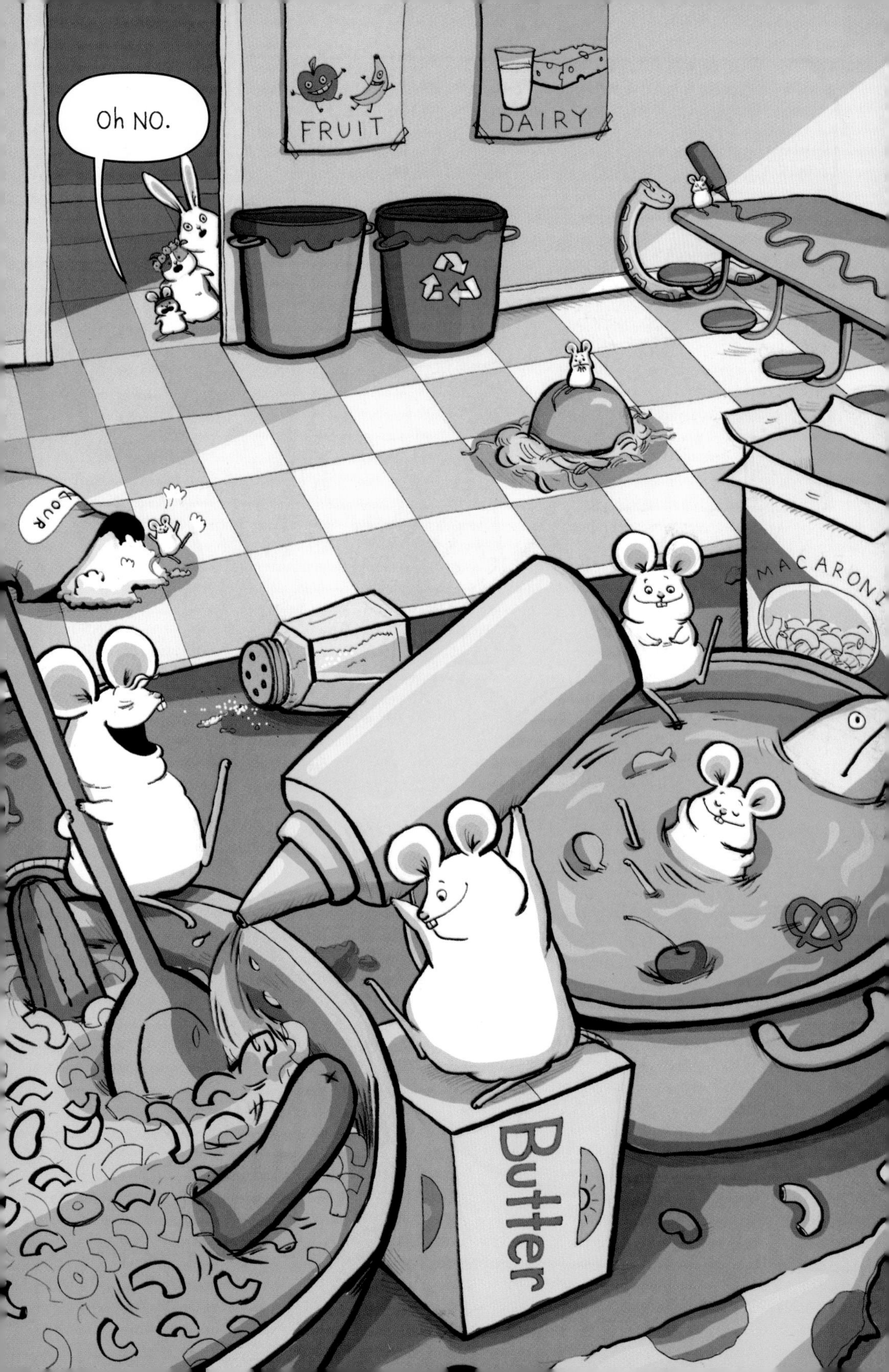
Oh NO.
FRUIT
DAIRY
MACARONI
Butter

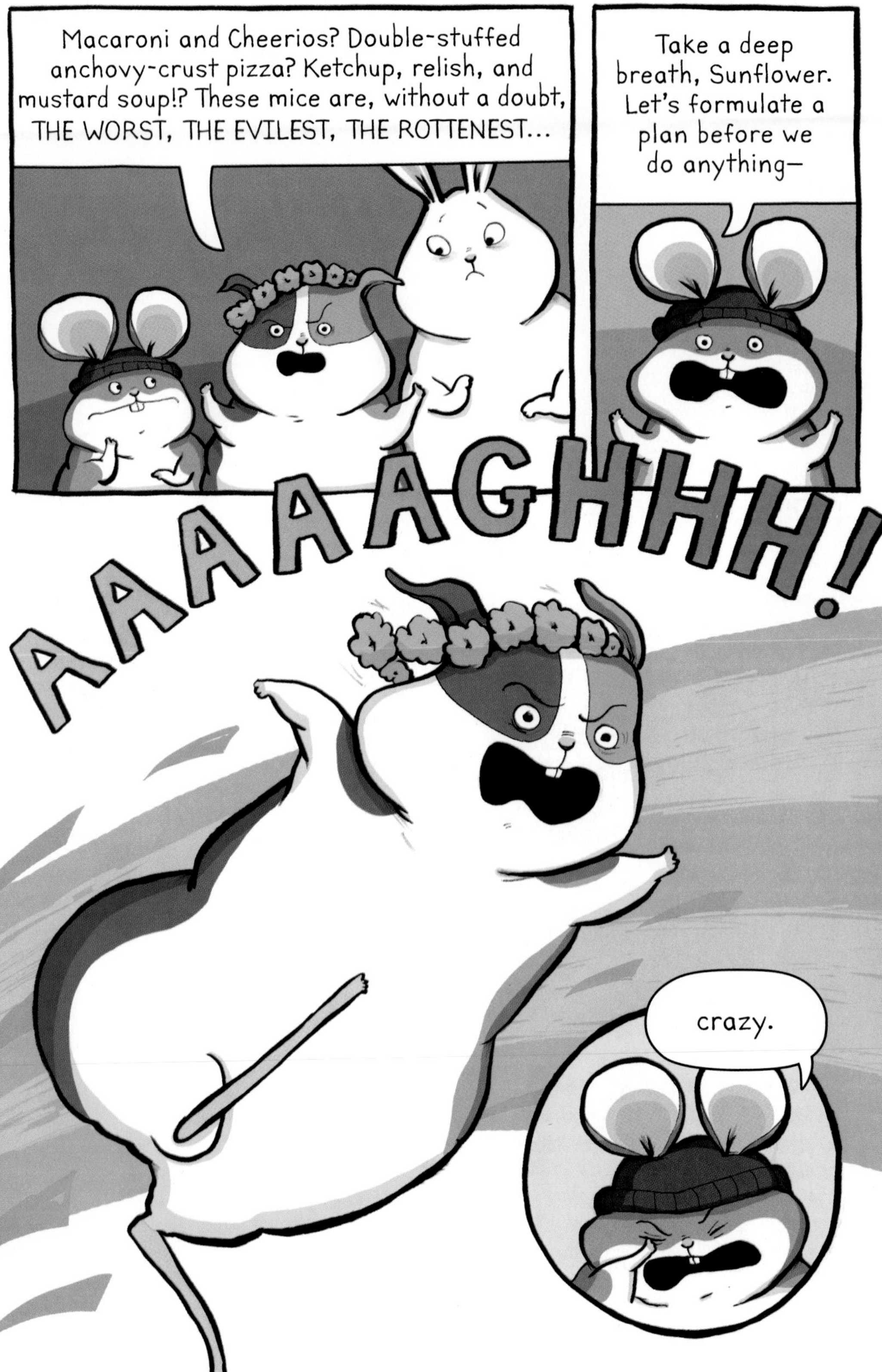
Macaroni and Cheerios? Double-stuffed anchovy-crust pizza? Ketchup, relish, and mustard soup!? These mice are, without a doubt, THE WORST, THE EVILEST, THE ROTTENEST...
Take a deep breath, Sunflower. Let's formulate a plan before we do anything—
AAAAAAGHHHH!
crazy.

49

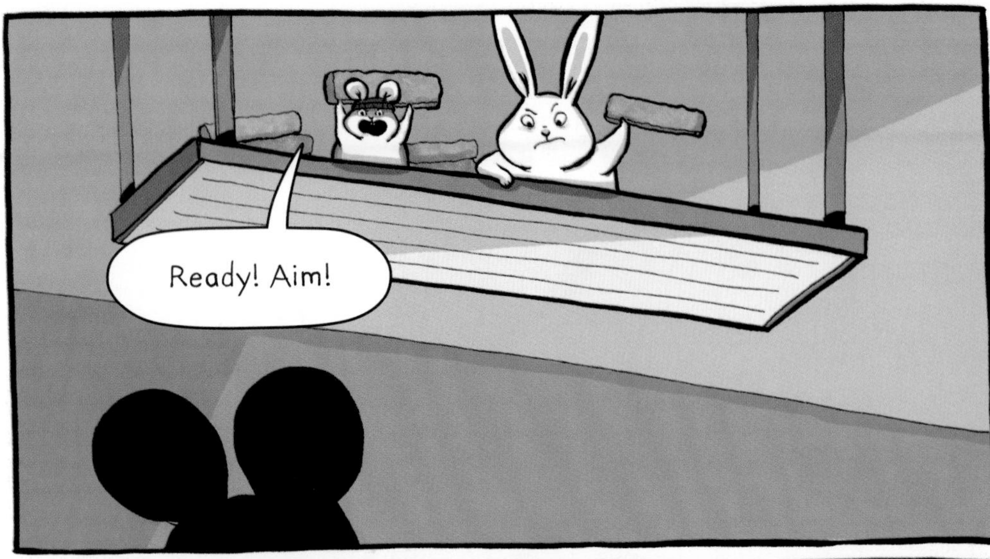
Ready! Aim!

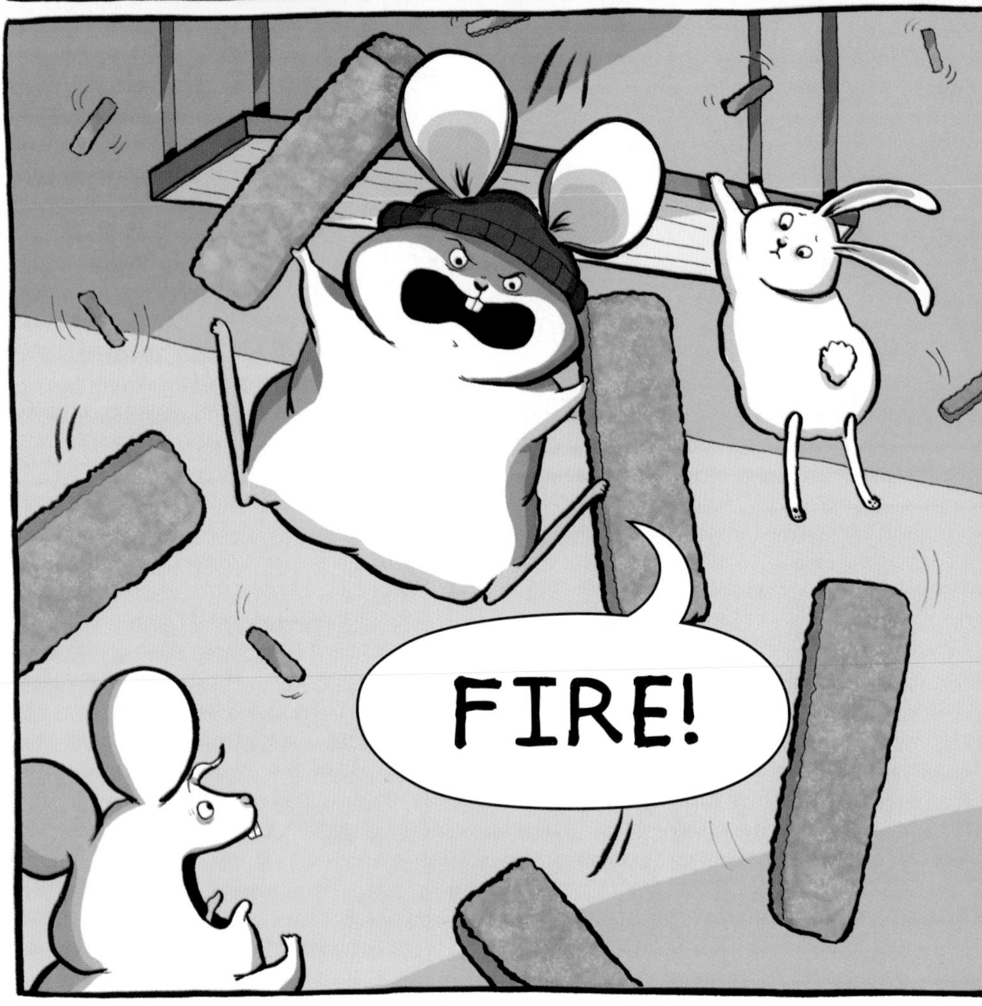
FIRE!

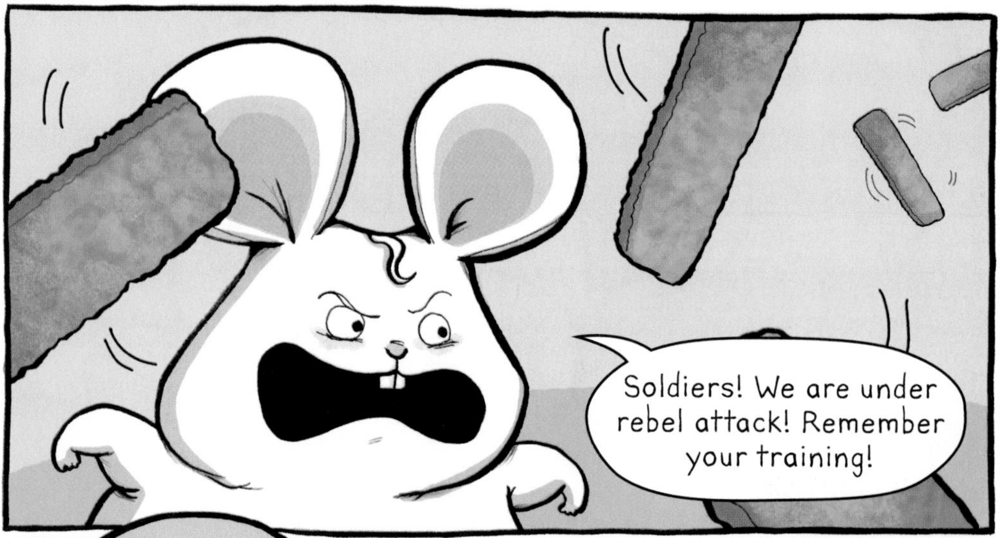
Soldiers! We are under rebel attack! Remember your training!

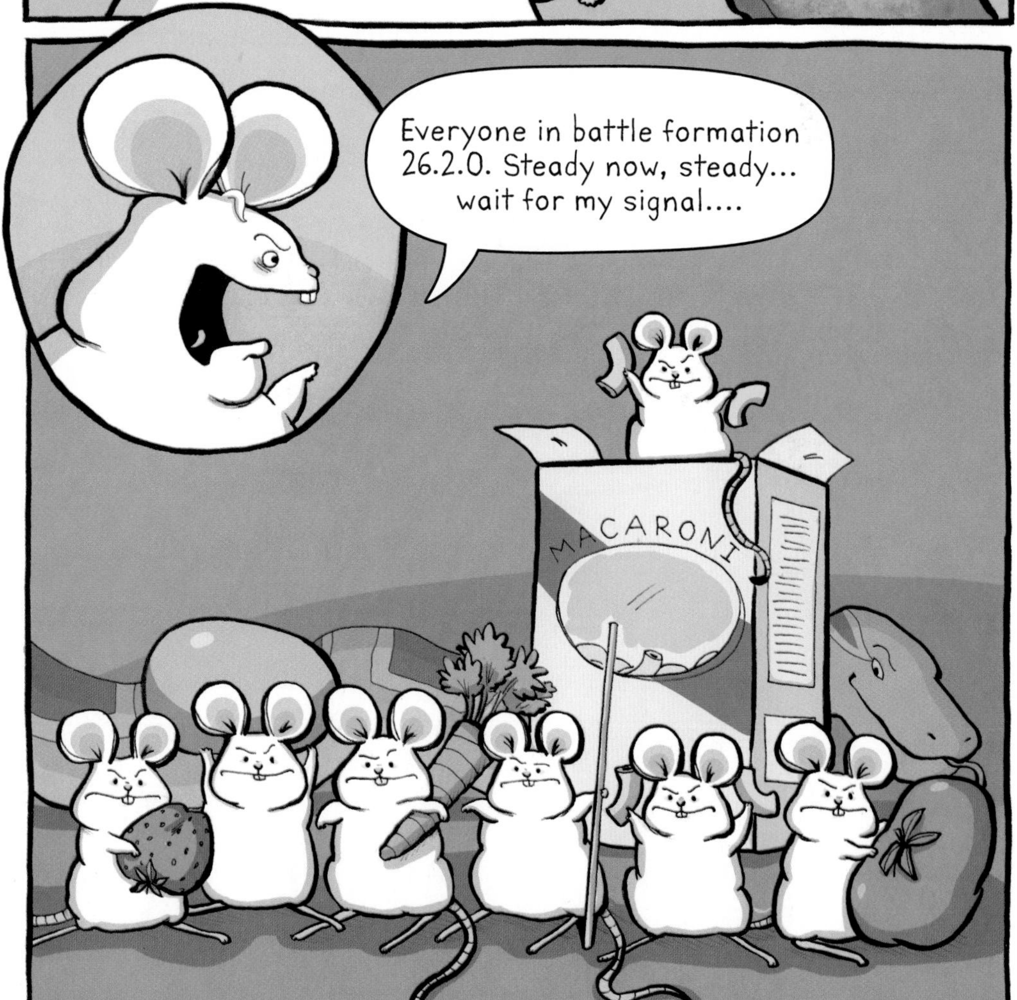
Everyone in battle formation 26.2.0. Steady now, steady... wait for my signal....
MACARONI

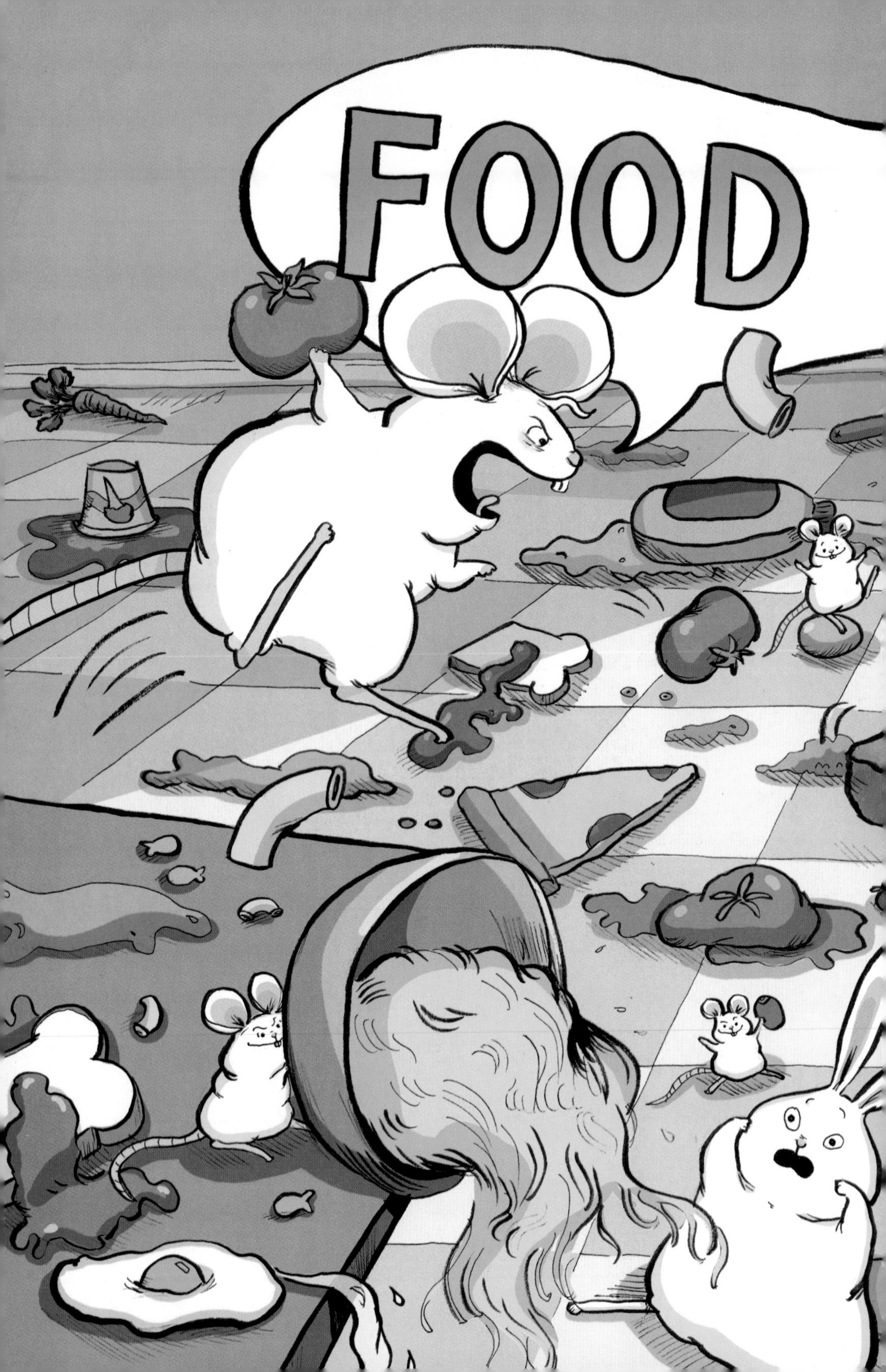
FOOD

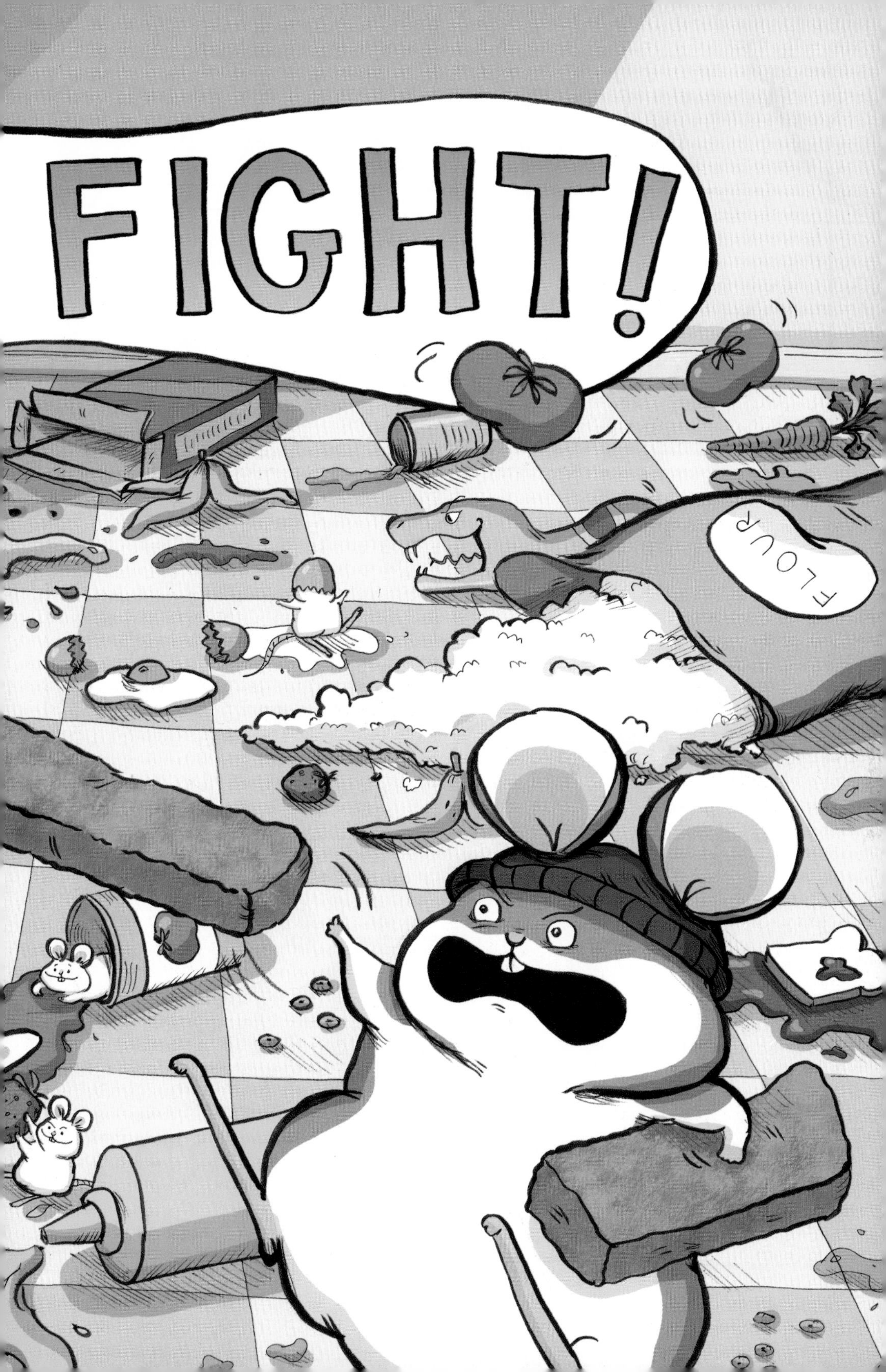
FIGHT!
FLOUR

Chapter 9

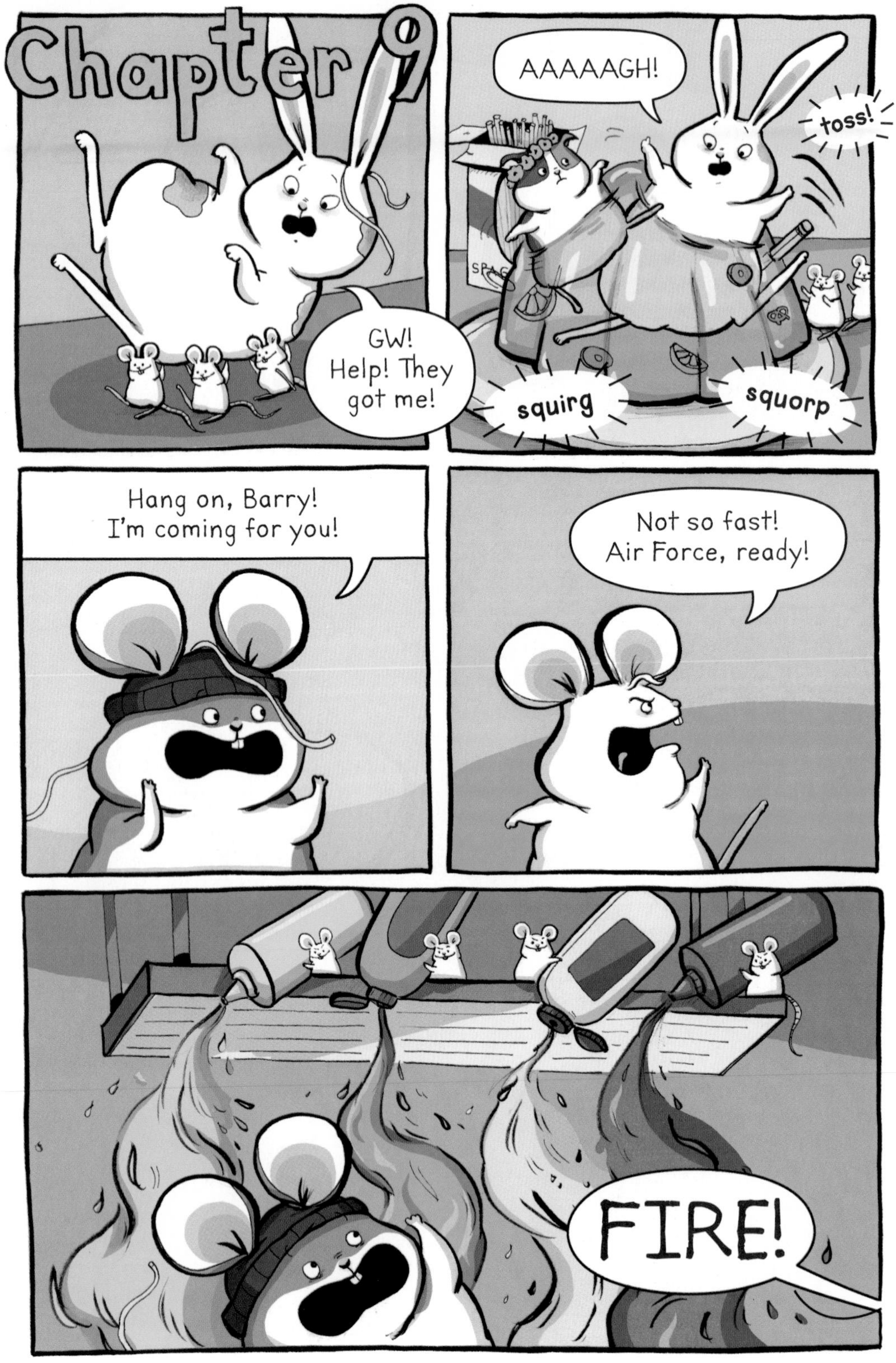
GW! Help! They got me!
AAAAAGH!
toss!
squirg
squorp
Hang on, Barry! I'm coming for you!
Not so fast! Air Force, ready!
FIRE!

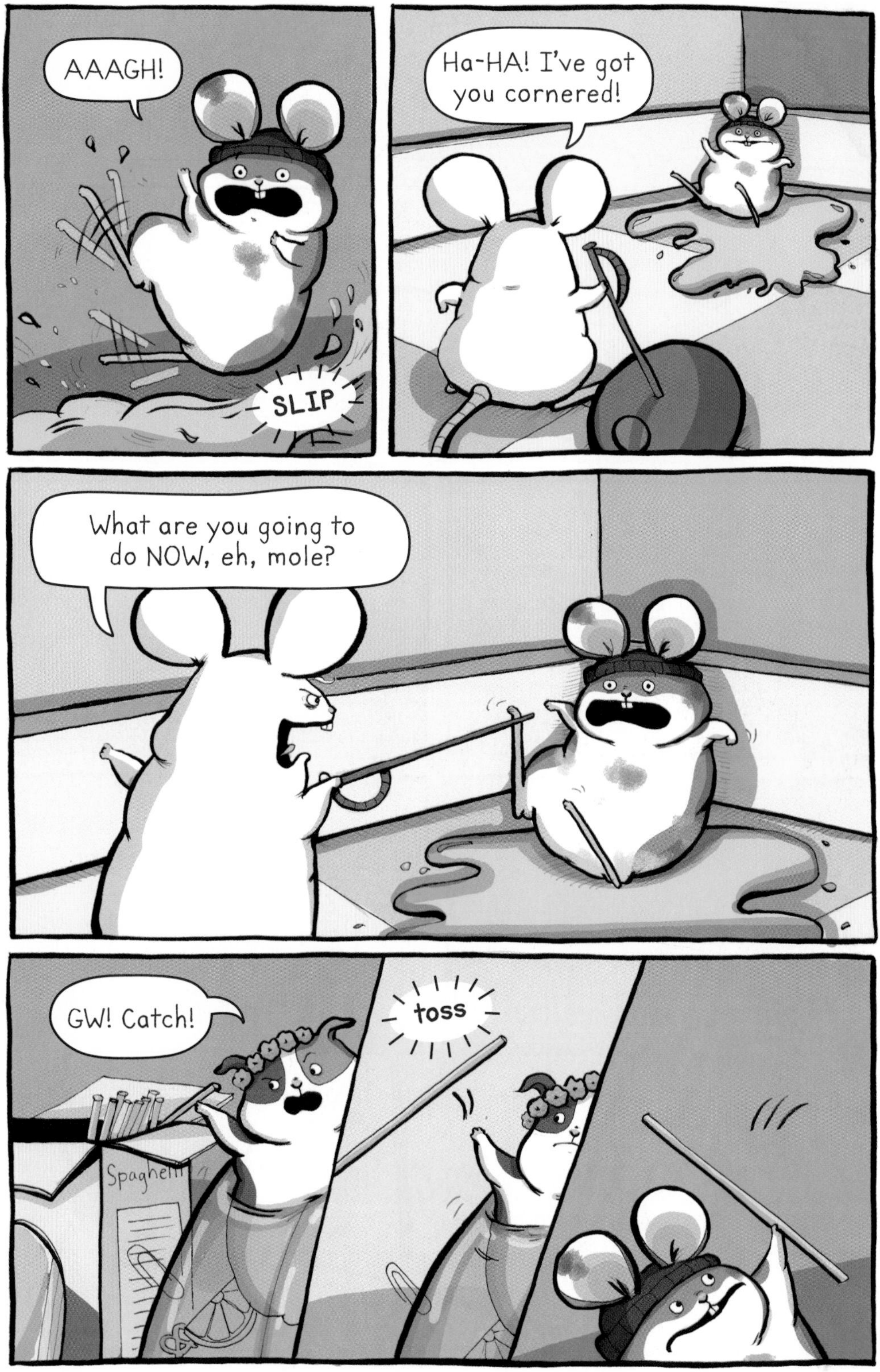
AAAGH!
SLIP
Ha-HA! I've got you cornered!
What are you going to do NOW, eh, mole?
GW! Catch!
toss
Spaghetti

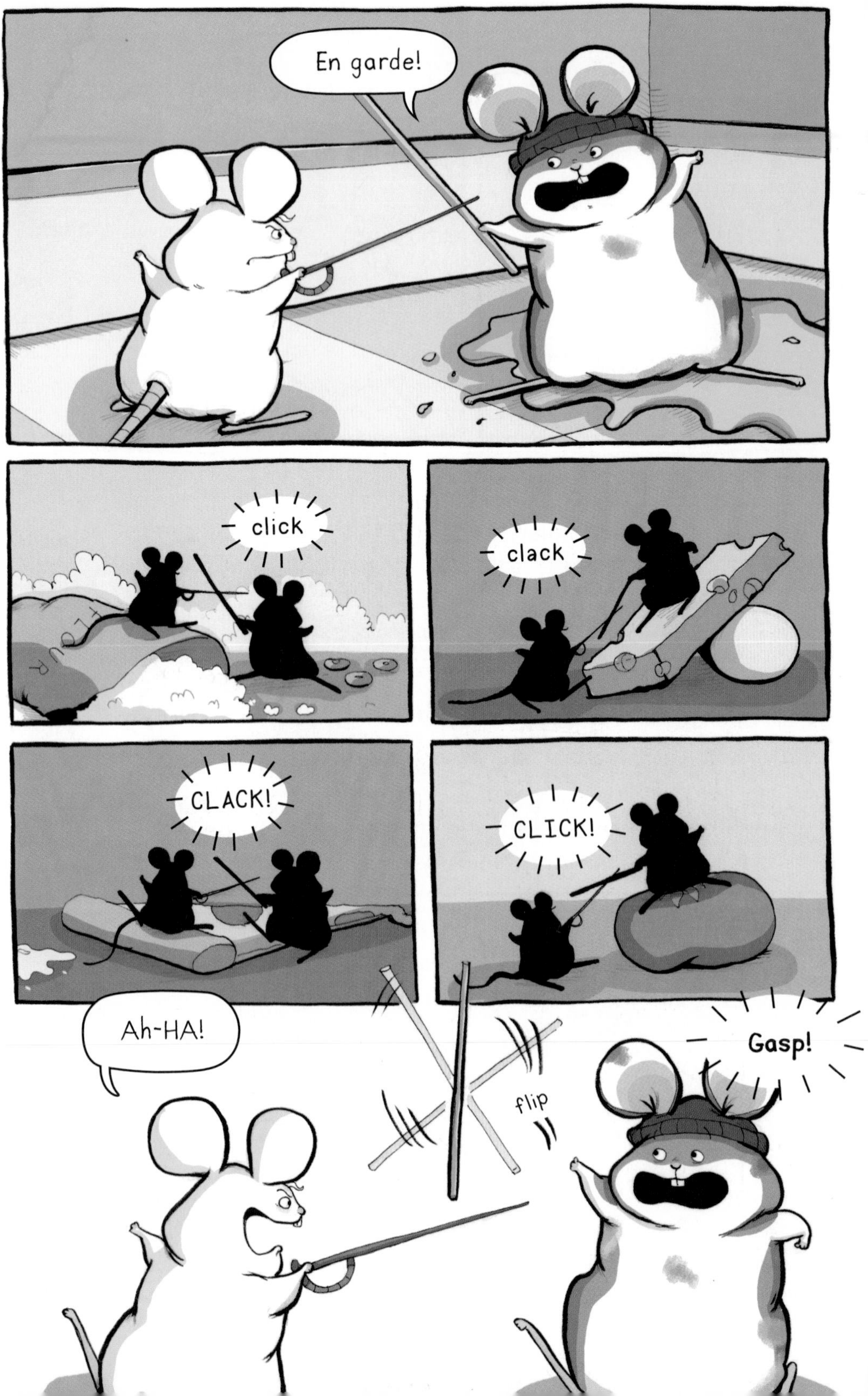
En garde!
click
clack
CLACK!
CLICK!
Ah-HA!
flip
Gasp!

57

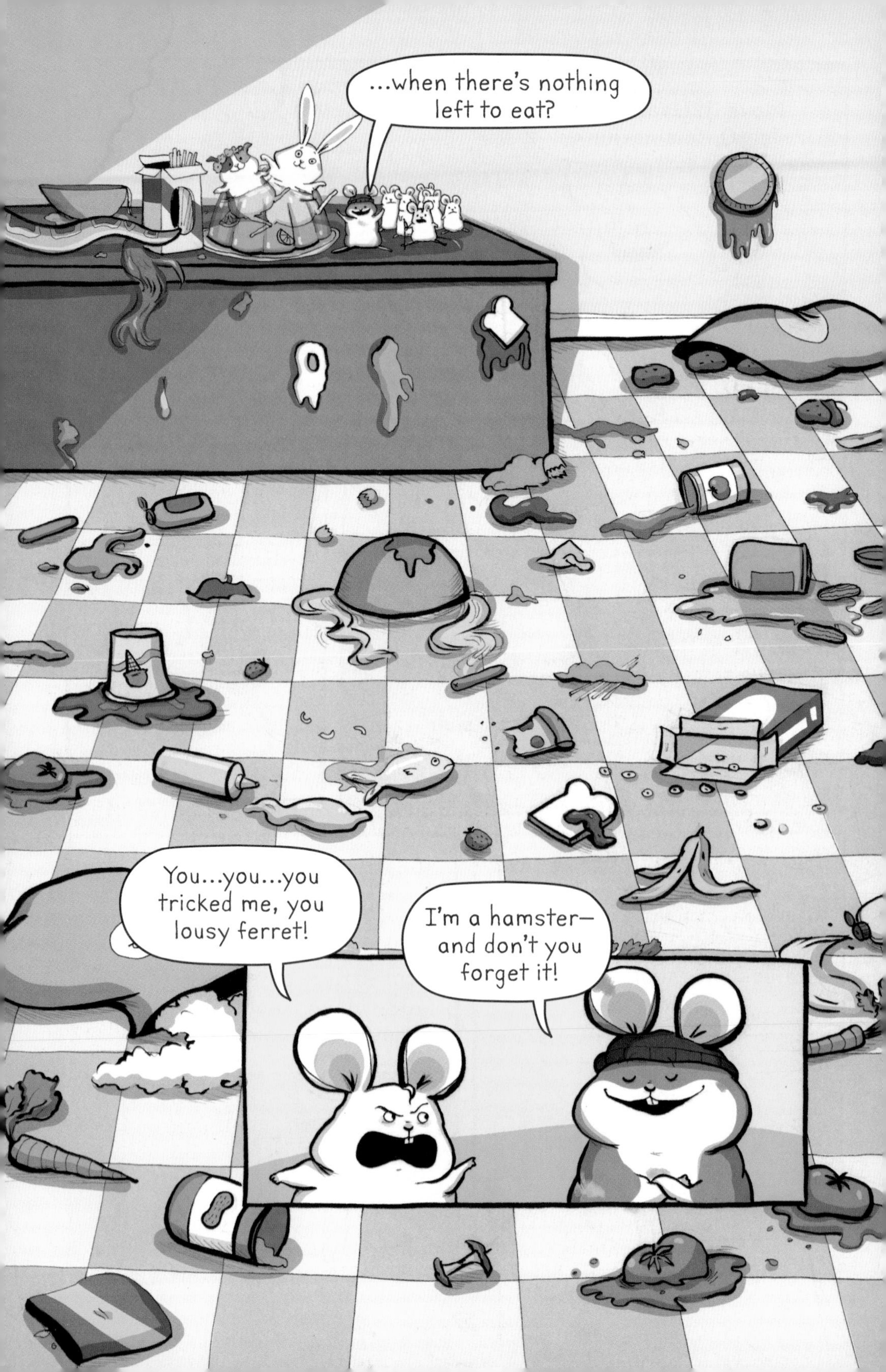
...when there's nothing left to eat?
You...you...you tricked me, you lousy ferret!
I'm a hamster—and don't you forget it!

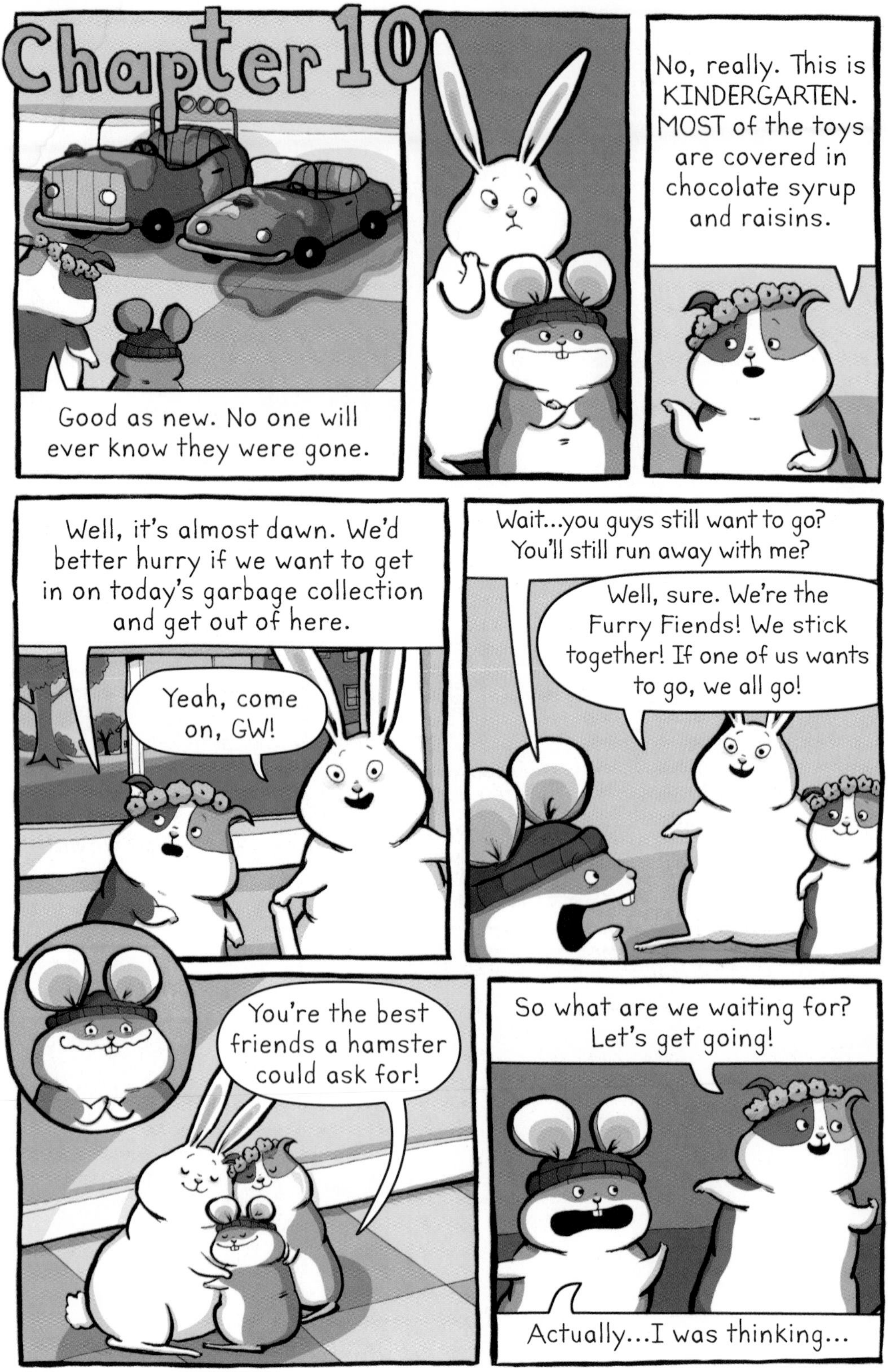
Chapter 10
Good as new. No one will ever know they were gone.
No, really. This is KINDERGARTEN. MOST of the toys are covered in chocolate syrup and raisins.
Well, it's almost dawn. We'd better hurry if we want to get in on today's garbage collection and get out of here.
Yeah, come on, GW!
Wait...you guys still want to go? You'll still run away with me?
Well, sure. We're the Furry Fiends! We stick together! If one of us wants to go, we all go!
You're the best friends a hamster could ask for!
So what are we waiting for? Let's get going!
Actually...I was thinking...

Chapter 11

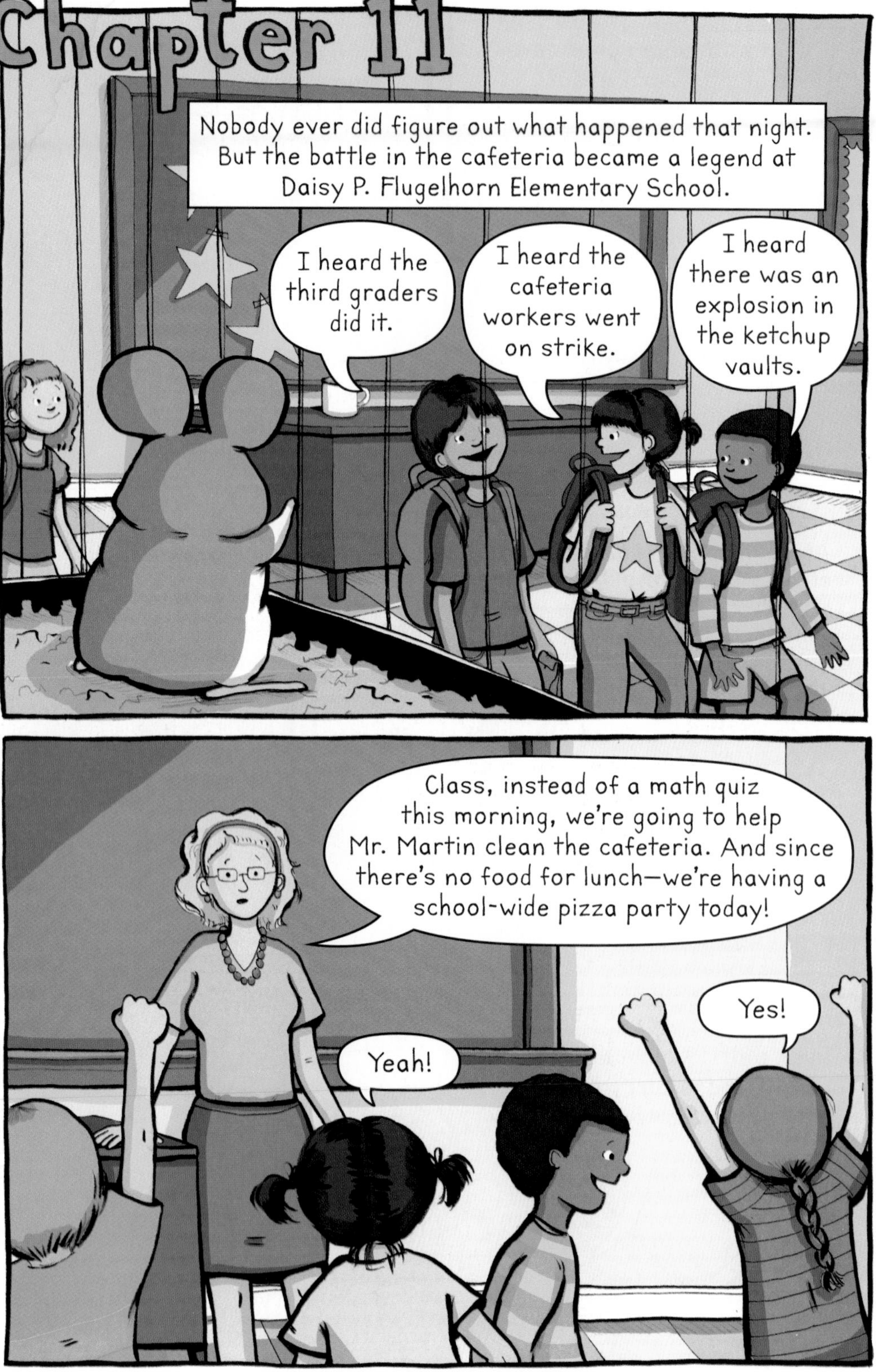
Nobody ever did figure out what happened that night. But the battle in the cafeteria became a legend at Daisy P. Flugelhorn Elementary School.
I heard the third graders did it.
I heard the cafeteria workers went on strike.
I heard there was an explosion in the ketchup vaults.
Class, instead of a math quiz this morning, we're going to help Mr. Martin clean the cafeteria. And since there's no food for lunch—we're having a school-wide pizza party today!
Yeah!
Yes!

For Oscar, my little mouse

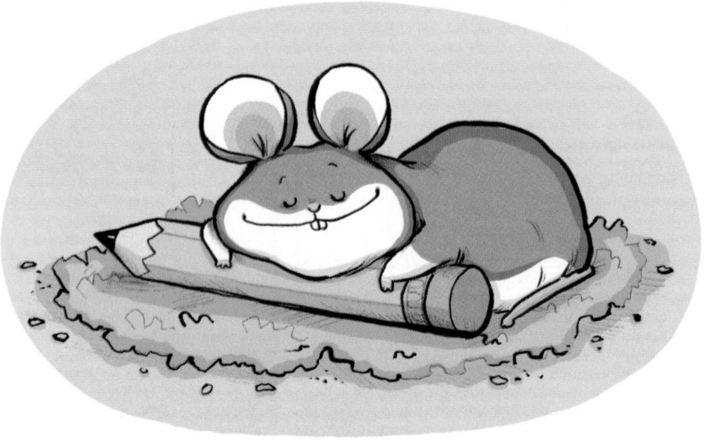

ISBN 978-1-338-03485-1

Published by Scholastic Inc., 557 Broadway, New York, NY 10012,
by arrangement with Henry Holt and Company, LLC.

12 11 10 9 8 7 20 21

Printed in the U.S.A. 40

First Scholastic printing, March 2016

The illustrations for this book were created with pen and ink; color was added digitally.